WHITE SHARK

This book is dedicated to:

Claire Barras

Donna Honig

Kevin Lavimodiere

Kathy O'Sullivan

Dave Picton

Ali Price

Simon Price

G Walker Smith

See you on the Vineyard!

WHITE SHARK

A Martha's Vineyard Mystery

By

Crispin Nathaniel Haskins

1

Red and white lights flashed onto the bedroom ceiling. For one brief instant, they made no sound in their unnaturally bright and colourful hip-hop across the drywall. They barely disturbed the two men in their single beds. Charles, in the bed furthest from the door, opened his eyes and watched them dance above him in a ritual his semi-lucid brain couldn't comprehend. Then almost immediately, the lights were joined by the scream of tires tearing across pavement. Rubber hollered in its battle between movement and direction. It felt like the windows of the house had shattered inward with the cacophony, shattered like they did in a bad horror movie, shattered in a detonation. The room filled with an explosion of sound, a cracking, crunching, and mechanical sound. Then, as quickly as it came, it was all sucked away in a vacuum of silence.

"What the hell was that?" Brad asked from his bed. He didn't expect a response.

Charles lunged out of bed, opened the bedroom door, and ran down the stairs. He took a brief second to put on his flip-flops, grateful that he had decided to sleep in boxers and a t-shirt. Brad came down the stairs behind him. Charles turned and looked at his friend. Brad's face looked unsettled, pale and yellow. Charles wondered if his face looked the same, like eggs in mid-scramble, not yet congealed. He decided that it probably did. After shouting to Brad to call 911, Charles ran into the night.

The porch light on their rental house lit the front lawn, the driveway, and the trees at the property line. Past that, there was an unfathomable blackness lit by nothing at all. Charles ran toward the road. His body coursed with adrenaline. His heart pounded in his ears. Wet dew from the lawn brushed onto his feet. It felt cold and made his flip-flops slippery. As he ran, Charles searched for any sign of the car or cars that had wakened him. Any sign that the whole thing hadn't actually been a terrible nightmare. He knew it wasn't. He might not have been so sure if Brad hadn't heard it too, but he had. If it was a nightmare, he was still in it. Reaching the end of the drive, Charles stopped and tried to let his eyes adjust. The light from the porch could accompany him no further. It had stretched out in its support as far as it could go. He was on his own. No birds chirped at this time of night. If the crash had disturbed them, they did not let on. There wasn't even the buzz of crickets. It was too early in the season. The days were plenty warm in June on Martha's Vineyard—Charles had even been swimming that afternoon—but the nights were still quite cool.

Charles looked deep into the black. Far on his left, he saw a single red light. A taillight? It looked like a taillight. He ran up the road toward it. As he got closer the light began to fade. Charles quickened his pace. The light flickered. Charles ran faster. His heart pumped. He didn't want to lose that beacon. The light peaked in the orange-red of a cigarette coal glowing on the last, long drag before being dropped and rubbed out under a boot. The taillight burned and then was gone. Charles stopped short in the dark. His beacon was gone. His legs were gooseflesh. A cold current of night air ran over him. The hair on his arms and neck lifted, rolled fluidly like algae on a riverbed. Charles shuddered. He turned to look back at the still lit driveway, now over a hundred feet behind him. It was the only thing discernable in the blackness. Seeing it was the only reassurance that Charles could find. He no longer knew exactly where he was going but he still knew how to get home. Turning back around, Charles faced the point where he believed the red light had been. He ran in that direction.

"Hello!" Charles yelled into the wall of darkness in front of him. There was no moon. No stars. He could barely see his hand in front of his face but he had to keep going. There was someone out there, maybe more than one person, who also couldn't see their hand in front of their face, someone who was not only as blind in the dark as he was but someone who was also bleeding to death. Someone who was pinched between a dashboard and a seat, scared, and not sure if they were going to survive what had just happened to them. "Is there anyone out there?" Charles yelled again. He found a great deal of comfort in hearing his own voice. His left foot went down and found something big, heavy but not solid ground. He felt a sharp pain in his toe and a sickening wrench in his ankle. He pulled his foot back reflexively and tried to regain his balance. Charles stumbled and flailed hitting something hard with his fist. He hopped twice and then found his footing. His ankle hurt and he slowed. It must be car parts, he thought. He was walking through bits of the wreckage. He slowed his pace. He heard pieces of plastic and metal scrape on the road under his feet. Charles was grateful that whatever he was stepping on wasn't wet and mushy. He didn't want to step in flesh. As long as it wasn't flesh. His heart raced faster at the thought. His imagination had always been far too vivid. He saw

10

his flip-flop sliding on sheets of skin, slices of scalp. His foot tickled by bits of hair. He imagined his foot splashed, not with the coolness of the night dew, but with the warmth of blood, his flip-flop becoming sticky instead of slippery. What was he running into? What would he do when he found someone? He was *going* to find someone. That was inevitable. Cars don't hurl themselves down the road in the middle of the night. Well, Stephen King's Christine had, but she was a satanic Plymouth. Satan's car didn't crash in the middle of the road. Satan was a better driver than that. Whoever was out in the blackness in front of Charles was hurt and needed help.

"Hello?" Charles called again.

"It's me! I'm the one!"

Charles jolted back. He heard and saw the man all at once. A young black man swayed out of the darkness toward Charles. By the time Charles could see him, he was no more than six feet away. He started to back up at the same pace that the man came toward him. Charles led him in the direction of the driveway light.

"What's your name?" Charles asked, slowly backing away.

"Sam Grover...my name is Sam Grover." The man seemed to think long and hard on this question. He breathed heavily. He kept walking toward Charles.

Charles didn't want to get too far away from the wreck but he didn't want to leave this man alone either. "Do you have some identification? Show me some ID please, Sam." Charles wanted to confirm that the man was thinking clearly, that he at least knew who he was.

"My mom! My mom is sick. I'm so sorry. It's all my fault." Sam Grover pulled a wallet out of the back pocket of his jeans and handed it to Charles. Charles held it toward the light from the drive and squinted to read it in the dark. Indeed, he was Sam Grover. Charles decided that Sam was thinking rationally. He returned the wallet and took Sam by the shoulder; it was too dark to get a really good look at him. He led him to the drive where the light was better.

"Sam! Focus on my voice for a minute please. Were you alone in the car? Is there anyone else in the car?"

"My mom is sick!" Sam said again. He was sweating and panting for breath. "I'm so sorry."

"Sam, is your mom in the car?" Charles held him firmly. It was too dark to see the extent of the damage but Sam's head was wet and shiny on one side. It looked like he could have quite a gash. Charles turned around and saw that Brad was still in the mouth of the driveway. Their friend Brooke was with him now. He yelled loud enough that Brad could hear him. "Brad, take Sam into the light and get a good look at his head.

Don't let him close his eyes! I'm going to see if there's anyone else in the car."

"Okay! Be careful!" The light from the house hit Brad sideways across his face. Charles could see Brad's eyes widen behind his glasses even at this distance. It looked like he had a thyroid condition.

Charles turned his attention back to Sam. "Sam, you have to go to my friend Brad over there. Do you see him? He's going to make sure that you are okay. Do you understand?"

Sam looked back into the darkness where Charles had first seen him. Then he looked down the road at Brad. "Okay. My mom's sick. I'm so sorry."

Charles watched the silhouette of Sam head down the road toward Brad and when he was sure that Brad had him, Charles turned back around and headed once more into the oily night. This time, as he ran, Charles braced himself not only to find a car wreck but also to find a sick woman inside it. Christ, he hoped she wasn't dead. What would he do if she were dead?

Charles continued into the black, once again feeling the bits of wreckage under the spongy soles of his flip-flops. The road turned and blindly he almost tripped over the edge. The earth fell away under his feet. Down the slope was a car lit only by the faint light on the inside of the passenger door. It had been impossible to see from a distance because the car was upside down. The driver's side, the side closest to

Charles, was crushed in completely. The door was completely concave, hammered in like a tin drum, indicating that the car had rolled on that side. How the hell Sam Grover had been able to walk out of this was beyond Charles. The passenger door was still open where Charles imagined that he had crawled out. The windshield was gone. Not smashed, gone. That was it. There was nothing else. It was a crushed-up car. There was no sign of a passenger. No sign of another car. Nothing at all to indicate that anyone other than Sam Grover had been in the accident at all. Had the mother been thrown? How the hell was he supposed to find her if she had been? There was nothing more that Charles could do at that time. Brad had called the emergency crew. They would certainly be better equipped to handle this than he was in his flip-flops, NHL boxers, and *JAWS* t-shirt. Charles scrambled back up to the road and headed toward the light that marked home.

Adrenaline still had his heart racing as he jogged into the driveway. The bright light made him wince after being in solid darkness for so long. There were three figures in the light. He could see his friends, Brad Park and Brooke Collins, standing with Sam Grover. Brad was talking to Sam and Brooke stood a few paces away. She looked frightened. Once in the drive, Charles slowed his jog to a walk. He needed to catch his breath. He tried to breathe deeply, to bring his heart rate down, but it was still racing. When he got close enough, he

14

could see the left side of Sam Grover's head. His temple was painted red and sticky; dirt and bits of leaves were glued to the open wound in a grisly decoupage. It was impossible to see exactly how bad the wound was without cleaning it up first. At the very least, Charles was happy that he was standing up and awake.

"He keeps trying to leave," Brad said matter-of-factly to Charles.

Charles shook his head. "No, I'm sorry. You can't leave. You've been in an accident. You're not going anywhere until you see a medic and speak to the police."

Sam's eyes widened. "No! No police! I have to go. My mom's sick."

"What do you mean your mom's sick? Where is she?" Charles was less concerned and more irritated at the mention of his ill mother than he had been at the crash site. When Charles had first heard of her, he had assumed that the woman was lying in a pool of her own blood, faeces, and vomit in a car that reeked of gasoline and was about to explode. Now, he was imagining some woman with the flu propped up in bed watching *The Tonight Show* with Jimmy Fallon.

"She just lives down the road. I have to go. I can't talk to the police." Sam Grover started down the driveway toward the street.

"Whoa! You can't. You need to speak to the police for your own protection if nothing else." Charles wasn't about to physically restrain him, but he figured he could slow him down until the emergency team got there.

"No! I have to go. My mom's house is just up here." Sam turned in the opposite direction from the crash and started jogging down the road. Charles stayed with him. He didn't run out in the middle of the night to save this guy only to have him collapse and die from a subdural haematoma in the middle of the street. And who's to say that the car he just rolled was even his? Nope. This guy was going nowhere—at least, not alone. They hadn't gone far when the lights of a fire truck, two police cars, and an ambulance appeared through the trees in front of them. There was no way out. The street they were on was a cul-de-sac. Charles stopped running.

"There. You have no choice now." Charles walked out into the middle of the road and started swinging his hands above his head in the universal signal for "stop". He stepped aside and stood where Sam had come to a halt. Sam was bent over with his hands on his knees trying to catch his breath, resigned to his fate. The first vehicle in the emergency convoy was the fire truck. It rolled up beside them, lights rolling, and the driver leaned out.

"You call about an accident?" the driver yelled out.

"You bet." Charles pointed toward the wreck. "Straight ahead."

"Anybody hurt?" the fireman asked.

"Just him." Charles jerked his thumb toward Sam. "He was the only one involved."

"No other car?"

"Not that I saw," Charles said.

"Okay. You stay and talk to the officer behind me." The truck drove on in search of the wreck, turning on a floodlight.

Two police cars drove up, followed by an ambulance. The cruisers stopped in a formation that blocked the two men in. Charles and Sam stood motionless. The officers' headlights blinded the two men. They winced. The red rolling lights were much less offensive, but the headlights were harsh. A short and stocky officer stepped out of the first car. He walked toward Charles without looking up. He pulled out a note pad and began to flip through it looking for an empty page. "I'm Sergeant Jack Burrell. Are either of you two gentlemen hurt?"

Charles smiled at the officer who he had come to know so well during his last visit. "He is. He's the one from the accident. I'm staying up the road. My friend called in the accident." Charles' grin broadened as he waited to be recognised.

With a jerk of his head, Sergeant Burrell motioned to Sam, still focused on his notes. "You talk to the officer over there. She's going to take you to the ambulance." He turned back toward Charles. "I have a few questions for you, sir. What's your name?"

Charles looked at the officer incredulously. "Jack! It's me!"

For the first time, the sergeant looked up and stared at Charles. "Charles Williams?"

2

"Laurie's going to kill me!" For the second time in four hours, Charles flew out of bed with a start. Once again the room was full of light but this time the light was natural and soft. The day was warm and bright and the bedroom was pulling it in from all sides. Three of the walls had windows and the longest wall, the east side of their rental house, was getting baked with the morning sun.

"What's the matter?" Brad lifted his head groggily from his pillow.

"Shit! Sorry bud. I'm late meeting Laurie! We're going for breakfast at the ArtCliff Diner and then we have to meet somebody about—" Charles stripped out of his boxers and t-shirt and put on a pair of tan cargo shorts and a turquoise polo shirt. They didn't smell the freshest—he had worn them the day before—but they didn't stink either. Charles hoped that Laurie wouldn't notice.

"About what?" Brad asked.

"What?"

"Meeting somebody about what?"

"Oh, damn it, I have no idea. Some sort of wedding crap." Charles ran into the adjoining bathroom to brush his teeth. He looked in the mirror. He really should have shaved. Laurie would think that he wasn't taking the wedding seriously and that wasn't the case at all. He just hadn't planned on spending the night running through the woods in his flip-flops rescuing strangers from rolled cars.

"Some sort of wedding crap? You're not going to call it that in front of Laurie are you? Somehow, I don't think that will go over well. I don't know her as well as you do but that's my gut feeling." Brad sat up and stretched. He looked around the room like he had never seen it before. "Looks like a nice day." He was waking up now.

Charles looked at Brad. Brad looked like crap too, but he didn't have to meet his fiancée in twenty minutes and the caterer in an hour. "That's it! She's the caterer!"

"Why do you need to meet with the caterer? You'll eat anything."

"I know! I *do* eat anything. Actually, I usually eat *everything* but that's a discussion for another time. I'm not sure why I have to be there. Laurie wants me there, though. Women are so weird. They want to feel like their men are excited and interested in the decision-making process of every minutia of the marital celebration but they will only accept the man's opinions if they're the same as their own. So if the groom-to-be sits back in what he deems to be the ultimate gift to his girlfriend and says, 'whatever you like honey, you can plan whatever you want,' he gets shot down for being an uncaring shmuck!" Charles was hopping around to keep his balance while he tried to pull on a sock. "So, *unofficially* I have no opinion, but *officially* I have to be there to give an opinion on every aspect of this wedding. I'm really surprised at Laurie. I didn't take her for that kind of girl at all. She's not a girlie-girl. I didn't think she'd go in for all of this wedding stuff."

"Indeed." Brad stared at his friend grimly. "Buddy, you can't go like that. You look like you've been running around in the woods all night." Brad chuckled at his own weak joke. "What was that all about anyway? Did that even happen? Crazy." He shook his head. "Get in the shower, shave for Christ's sake, and put on clean clothes. I'll drive you. You'll be fine."

Charles exhaled every bit of breath in him. He threw the sock across the room. His shoulders dropped about four inches. He felt like he had been given electroshock therapy and the treatment just ended. "Thanks man. That's awesome. Give me ten minutes."

*   *   *

Charles stepped out of Brad's green Subaru Outback and onto the unmarked gravel that served as the Art Cliff Diner's parking lot. It was early but the diner was already quite busy. In high season, it was near impossible to get in without a wait unless you got there promptly when it opened at seven-thirty. Charles closed the car door behind him with just enough force to hear the mechanical click of the latch. He leaned down and peered in the open window. "Thanks again man. I really owe you."

"Don't worry about it. It was good to get me out of the house."

"Why don't you come in and have breakfast? My treat. It's the least I can do. In fact, better yet, I'll make Laurie pay for both of us!" Charles grinned. "What do you say?"

Brad chuckled. "No, you guys have things to discuss. I'm going to go and wake up Brooke. I want to go and check out the breakfasts you keep talking about at The Edgartown Inn. We'll go down there before it gets too busy. I like walking around Edgartown in the morning. Text me later and we'll hook up."

"Sounds like a plan. Say 'hi' to Edie for me. Tell her I sent you." Charles smiled again.

"Will do." Brad put the car into gear and it began to slowly roll forward. The wheels growled in the gravel as they found traction.

Charles stepped back and watched his friend drive into the sparse, early morning traffic on Beach Road. He gave one last wave as the Subaru headed toward Oak Bluffs before he turned and walked toward the front door of the diner.

"The Art Cliff Diner Est. 1943" read the large, pop-art sign on top of the restaurant. It was a bright, welcoming sign of yellow, red, and blue. Charles had always loved the juxtaposition of the primary colours. Maybe it was a childhood thing. People always learned them first. The sign was really the only thing that stood out on the building. The rest of it was the island standard. It was pretty, but very simple and straightforward—a weather-greyed, cedar-shingled bungalow with white trim. White posts held up the roof over the porch and there were clay pots filled with evergreen plants, flowers, and American flags at the base of each post. A bright red screen door let the fresh morning air in and kept the summer insects out. Charles stepped up to the red door and opened it. The metal spring yawned in weak protest and pulled the door closed behind him with a light *thwap*.

Laurie was sitting on his right at a table for two in the corner. She was reading the newspaper. Her hair was pulled back into a ponytail, as was her custom when she was off duty. Her running shoes were white and she wore dark blue jeans and a pink Black Dog sweatshirt—she looked fresh and bright. Charles was glad that he had showered, shaved, and put on clean clothes. Standing in his bedroom he had thought he looked all right in his previously worn, rumpled clothes, and his unshaven face. Standing beside her in the ArtCliff Diner he would have looked homeless.

"Good morning." Charles leaned in to kiss her.

"Good morning yourself." Laurie tilted her head back to meet his kiss. They both smiled.

Charles pulled out the chair opposite her and sat down.

With her right hand, Laurie gestured to the waitress for more coffee. She looked across the table at Charles. "How are things at the fraternity house?"

Charles laughed. "It's not a fraternity house. Brooke's there too. So is Tina. It's not an entirely male realm."

"I know. Don't remind me. I must be the most understanding bride-to-be in the world. My fiancé is staying in a rental house with other women. Unbelievable." Laurie shook her head.

"Consider it my bachelor party." Charles grinned at her in his best Cheshire cat impression.

24

"Oh, I am. Believe me. I think it's kind of cool actually. It will make it a lot easier when we get to the night before the wedding. You're going to need a place to stay and you may as well be staying with your friends. They came a long way."

"Some." Charles nodded.

"So when are you going to tell me about this?" Laurie folded the paper, so that the lower right-hand corner of the front page was facing up. She passed it to him.

Charles read the headline, *Youth Rolls BMW In Oak Bluffs*. "Oh that." He grinned. "I was getting around to it."

Laurie raised an eyebrow. "I'm actually surprised you made it here on time this morning."

"You have Brad to thank for that. I almost didn't." Charles rolled his eyes.

"Thank you, Brad," Laurie said.

Their waitress came and set an Art Cliff mug in front of Charles. She poured from her coffee pot until the steaming, dark, rich brew was a half an inch from the rim. "Are you guys ready to order or do you need a couple of minutes?"

Laurie looked up at her. "I know what I want, Heather, but my friend might need a couple more minutes."

Heather refilled Laurie's mug.

Charles shook his head. "Nope! I'm good."

"Oh! Okay." Laurie looked up at Heather, whose bright, freshly scrubbed young face looked genuinely happy to be there to help them. "I'd like the Mr T frittata please, with white toast."

"Awesome choice, Chief." Heather nodded her approval. She looked at Charles.

"I'll have the same," he said.

"Awesome! That's easy! Two Mr Ts coming right up! White toast too?"

"Yes please," Charles said. "Oh, a grapefruit juice too, please."

"Make that two," Laurie added. She handed Heather their menus.

"You got it!" Heather spun on her heel and bounced away to put in their order.

Laurie looked back at Charles and tapped her finger on the news story. "You were saying?"

Charles picked up the newspaper and read the story. It only took a minute. Charles was a quick reader and the story was short. There wasn't much of a story, wasn't much to write. Essentially, the headline said it all. "I'm not even mentioned! They missed the human-interest angle." Charles slipped into an overly dramatic news anchor voice. "Fearless tourist plunges into the darkness to help injured stranger!"

"Oh please." Laurie rolled her eyes.

"That would have been a much better story." Charles handed the paper back to Laurie, picked up his coffee and took a deep gulp. He regretted it immediately; the coffee was still really hot. He grimaced. "Seriously though, if I wasn't mentioned in the story, how did you know that I was involved at all?" As soon as he heard the question out loud, he knew the answer. They answered in unison.

"Jack!" they said.

Charles nodded. "Of course."

"Of course. We, the police, have a habit of letting each other know when family members are involved in car accidents in the middle of the night. Cops are funny like that." Laurie sipped her coffee.

The design on the side of her mug was a condensed version of the sign on top of the restaurant. Charles checked his own mug. His was the same. He liked it. He wondered how much they were. He assumed they were for sale. Almost everything was for sale on the Vineyard, or it seemed that way to Charles anyway. Economies that relied on seasonal tourism were like that.

Heather brought their grapefruit juice and left wordlessly.

"So, what happened? Are you going to tell me or not?"

Charles told her the story from being awakened by the car lights and screeching tires to following Sam Grover down the street as he tried to avoid the police. Laurie listened intently. She didn't interrupt. She trusted his instinct to tell her the meat and to cut away the fat of the story. When he finished, he stopped for a moment and thought.

Heather returned with their food. "Here you go, Two Mr T frittatas! Do you need anything else? Ketchup? More coffee?"

"More coffee please, Heather, when you get a minute." Laurie asked.

"Absolutely, Chief."

Laurie looked down on the casserole dish that Heather set in front of her. Scrambled eggs layered over Yukon gold potatoes covered with slices of chorizo sausage, jalapeno peppers, and onion, all baked under pepper jack cheese. There was crisply toasted white bread on the side.

"This looks delicious!" Laurie said.

"Have you had this before?" Charles asked.

She shook her head. "No."

"Oh, well *it is* delicious."

"When did you have this?" Laurie eyed him quizzically.

"Two years ago when I was here for JAWSfest."

She nodded in acknowledgement.

Charles picked up a triangle of toast and took a bite. "You know what's odd?"

"The fact that you're here to marry me and you're shacked up in the middle of the woods with two other women?" Laurie raised an eyebrow and grinned mischievously.

Charles laughed. "You're a piece of work, you know that?"

"So I've been told." Laurie chuckled through a mouthful of chorizo sausage.

"I mean about last night." Charles took another bite of toast and washed it down with a swig of coffee. "I can't stop thinking about it."

"What?" Laurie asked.

Charles set down the remaining portion of toast and folded his hands in front of his face. "Sam Grover drove past our rental house and crashed his car off the bend just *east* of us. Okay?" He continued without waiting for a response. "When he came out of the dark, when he came running up to me, he kept apologising and saying that his mom was sick."

"You told me this already. So did Jack last night, as a matter of fact. That's not what you want to tell me. What else?"

"When he realised the police were on their way, he said he had to go to his mom's house. He said that she just lived down the road. With his head injury, I didn't want him to be left alone nor did I think he should leave without speaking to the police after rolling the car. So, I followed him down the driveway and then, he turned *west*, in the *opposite* direction of the crash site."

Laurie scooped up a heavily peppered triangle of egg and sausage and slipped it into her mouth. Her lips closed and she pulled the fork out cleanly. Laurie chewed for a few seconds and then picked up her glass and rinsed out her mouth with the fresh, sweet, tartness of the grapefruit juice. She cleared her throat. "So where was he driving in the first place?"

"Exactly."

3

Laurie drove through the intersection of Main and Water Streets in Edgartown. It was Charles' favourite place on the entire island. In his mind, it showcased the quintessential aesthetic of Vineyard life. Other than the red brick of the Edgartown Bank, all of the store edifices were wood, painted in nautical white. A leafy ceiling of trees was thick over Main Street. Pot lights of sun pierced through to the tourists and red brick sidewalks below. Charles had been coming to the island for forty years and in that time some of the stores had changed, and the signs had changed, but the storefronts had not. When a new merchant moved in, he or she hung a new shingle but that was all. Nothing changed on the Vineyard but the seasons. At least, that's how it seemed to an outsider, a mainlander. Charles knew that he would always be seen as a mainlander but he looked forward to the day when he would no longer be seen as an outsider. He wondered how long that would take. He wondered if Laurie was still an outsider. Would being a police chief divert attention from being an outsider or emphasise it? It was an interesting question, the answer to which would have a direct bearing on how the islanders saw him.

Laurie parked her cruiser at the bottom of Main Street by the Edgartown Yacht Club and the Atlantic Fish and Chop House. When Charles had first returned to the island and they had begun running around for the wedding, he had pointed out to her that she always parked in front of a restaurant. Laurie explained to him that she parked her car near a restaurant whenever she could. Her plan was always to do what needed to be done and then get lunch, dinner, or a snack; whichever was appropriate, if she was hungry. That way, when she was finished eating, the car was right outside when she was done. Because she usually started her errands at off-meal hours there was always a good parking spot available. On the other hand, if she tried to go somewhere for food when she was done, she would just end up hungry and pissed off because she couldn't park the car. Charles thought it was pretty smart.

"How long was it before the islanders no longer saw you as an outsider?" Charles asked as he stepped out of the cruiser and closed his door.

"Oh, am I no longer an outsider? I didn't even get a parade," Laurie deadpanned.

"Oh! Are you still an outsider?" Charles asked. "You've been here for years!"

Laurie walked over to him and took his hand. They started up Lower Main Street with their fingers intertwined.

"Well, the whole 'islander-non-islander' thing will never really change but it only seems to be an issue when people are upset. Happy people see me maybe not as an islander, but not as an outsider either and they would certainly never point it out with the same distain as an unhappy person would. I hear it jokingly on occasion at a party or something but that's about it. The only other time I hear it is if I'm locking up a drunk in the drunk-tank. He'll slur, 'You're not even an islanda' at me for sure. Then there are a few rich islanders who try to use me as a personal gofer. When I don't kow-tow to them, I get told that, 'my ignorance stems from not being an islanda.' What they hope to achieve by that exactly is beyond me. Insulting the police chief is never a good way to get her on your side. Why do you ask? Trying to figure out how long it's going to be before you get to become an islander? Well, in the immortal words of Fritzi Jayne Courtney, 'Nevah!

Nevah! You're not bawn heah, you're not an islanda! That's it.'"

Charles laughed out loud. "Your New England accent is terrible!"

"That's it? That's all you have to say? I throw a *JAWS* quote at you *and* throw in the name of the rather obscure actress who said it and all you can do is trash my accent? You're brutal!" Laurie unlaced her fingers from his and elbowed him in the stomach playfully.

Charles grabbed his stomach and yelped in pain. He was still laughing. "Alright! Alright! You win! I am very impressed with your quote. Actually, I am really impressed that you knew Fritzi's name. A lot of *JAWS* fans don't even know her name."

As they reached the corner of Water Street, Laurie took his hand once again.

"Well, I know that she's your favourite character."

"You do?" Charles was surprised.

"Of course I do!" Laurie huffed in exasperation. "Charles, what's my favourite movie and who's my favourite character?"

"Scarface. Tony Montana."

"See?" She grinned. "Why would my memory be any worse than yours?" She kissed him on the lips quickly. "Let's go. We're going to be late. Edie's probably there already."

"I didn't know that Edie was meeting us."

"Charles, Edie's the wedding planner." Laurie started across Water Street.

Charles followed her across Water and the two of them headed up Main Street in the early morning sun. Charles did his best to always walk on the sunny side of the street. The sun didn't shine every day; he figured it was always best to take full advantage of it when he could. "I know that. I just didn't think that she had to be there for every one of our decisions. I figured she would help set up appointments and keep track of everything but I didn't think that she had to be there all the time."

"She doesn't, I suppose, but we're not far from the inn and she wanted to say 'hi'. Besides, she likes all of this wedding stuff. More than some of us."

"What is that supposed to mean?" Charles asked. If she meant him, it was true; however, her comment made him defensive anyway.

"Nothing." Laurie continued up the street without looking at him. She had barely passed the ATM at the Edgartown Bank when Charles stopped walking. They were still hand in hand so it forced Laurie to turn around and stop, all in one motion.

"What's going on? Talk to me, Chiefy." Charles spoke warmly and softly.

"It's pretty clear that you're not very excited about this," Laurie said.

"I'm excited about you. I'm excited about marrying you. As long as I get to say that you are my wife when this is all over—I'm happy. That's all I want. If you want me to lose sleep over whether our tablecloths are ivory or ecru or the bridesmaids' dresses are blush or bashful pink, it's just not going to happen. It's not important to me. I know that it's important to you, so making sure that you get what you want is important to me. If you want magicians to pull live doves out of a monkey's ass, I say do it! If someone tries to stop you, call me and I'll take care of him or her for you. The really important thing for me is that *I get to marry you.* I walk around all day feeling like I won the goddamn lottery and when you win the lottery; you don't care if they give it to you in cash or cheque. You know what I mean?" Charles watched Laurie's eyes well up.

"I'm sorry. This wedding crap has me all messed up." Laurie wiped her eyes. "Christ, I'm such a girl!" She reached into her pocket and pulled out a tissue to wipe her nose.

"Nobody's perfect," Charles mocked.

Laurie elbowed him in the stomach again.

"Ouch!" Charles exclaimed. "I was just kidding!" He held his stomach with both hands. "You know, I think that's part of the problem?"

"What is?" Laurie looked at her watch and grabbed his hand again. "Come on, we really have to go."

"All this 'girly-girl' stuff is not usually your thing. I think that you feel a little out of your element and it's stressing you out."

Laurie stopped again. "Jesus, have you got me pegged. Charles, I feel like I'm flying by the seat of my pants!" Laurie sat down on one of the wooden benches that lined the street. Charles sat down beside her. "Every day, I make decisions on the lives of citizens. I break up bar fights, I arrest drug dealers, I answer calls of domestic abuse; being inundated with decisions about paper or cloth napkins, band or DJ, is just not my thing." Her eyes watered and she wiped away her tears with her tissue. It seemed to Charles that they were tears of exhaustion and embarrassment more than anything else. Before he spoke, he picked up her hand and held it in his.

"It doesn't matter." Charles looked at her and smiled thoughtfully.

Laurie looked at him incredulously. "Oh thanks a lot. That's just what I needed to hear; my running around to put on the perfect wedding has been a complete waste of time. Thank you. I feel bathed in relief."

"You're not wasting your time. I'm just saying don't sweat the small stuff, you know? Our wedding is going to be great. We're keeping it small. We love all of the people who are going, they all love each other, and some of them even like us."

Laurie chuckled.

"Now, I want you to do yourself a favour and let Edie take over in the planning. If she's coming to these little meetings then she doesn't have much to do. I know you, Laurie Knickles; you don't want to be a burden on Edie *and*, more importantly, you don't want to hand over the reins. Stop being such a control freak!"

Laurie sat back on the bench and looked across Main Street. An old man stood with his hands full of shopping bags waiting while his wife sized up yet another store window. She was deciding whether or not he had to go in that store too. Charles followed Laurie's gaze to the old couple and wondered if at some point all husbands just give up and do what they're told. Charles thought it would be awful to feel resigned to your life rather than to feel like you had an active part in it. Surely, that didn't have to happen. If a couple started out really communicating, he doubted that they ever stopped. Couples who said that they drifted apart never really knew each other in the beginning, in his estimation. Charles and Laurie sat in silence for a minute before Charles spoke again.

"What are we doing here today anyway?" Charles asked.

38

"Cake tasting." Laurie said calmly, watching the older woman across the street take her husband by the hand and walk away from the clothing store. "It should have been done ages ago, but with you living in Toronto the timing was tough. They're making an exception for me." The old man kissed his wife on the top of her head.

"The perks of marrying the Chief of Police." Charles smiled as he watched the older couple. He looked back at Laurie. "So we get to eat cake?"

"Yup."

"Alright, so let's go eat cake, tell the cake lady which one we want, give Edie the power of attorney over the rest of the wedding, and then go for a swim before lunch. What do you say?" Charles stood and held out his hand.

Laurie smiled up at him from the bench. Her eyes had cleared. She reached up and took his hand in hers. "You're on!"

*   *   *

The sun was shining brightly when the bells in the Old Whaling Church chimed twelve o'clock. On the sixth bell, Edie, Charles, and Laurie exited the caterer's office above Scoops Ice Cream and walked down the back stairs onto South Summer Street.

Charles and Laurie walked hand in hand toward Main Street. Edie walked alongside, busily scribbling onto a yellow pad. Her golden hair bobbed as she walked. Charles thought that Edie's hair always seemed to be in perpetual motion, her natural loose curl somehow spring-loaded. She walked with a confident stride in open-toe wedges. "Alright, you two. I really have to get back to work. The Edgartown Inn needs me!" She smiled broadly and her eyes squinted over her cheeks. "Where are you guys headed?"

"We're parked down by the Yacht Club," Laurie said.

"Oh, okay. I'll walk you down to Water Street." Edie scribbled a couple more things down onto her pad before stuffing it into her oversized black purse. She pulled the purse over her shoulder and then straightened her turquoise blouse and black cardigan. "I think lemon cake with vanilla crème icing was a good choice. It's simple. Everyone will like it. We can do the whole cake in an off-white and it will look quite elegant."

"Thanks Edie. I think so too." Laurie smiled.

There was a moment's pause before Edie spoke up again. "Don't you think it sounds elegant too, Charles?"

"I think it sounds delicious. You want me excited about a cake? Don't call it elegant, call it *big*!" Charles laughed. The women laughed too. Charles was relieved

40

that the mood had lightened considerably since their walk to the caterer.

"Men!" Edie rolled her eyes. "Stick them in a corner and give them a toy to play with."

"You say that as an insult but you're right, we'd be happy with that." Charles grinned. "The cake was delicious. I'm excited that we have that out of the way."

"There's really not that much more to do. Laurie, I know you're wound up like a three-dollar watch, but relax. All that's left are little odds and ends. I run an inn. I'm a multi-tasker. Making sure everyone's comfortable and well fed is my stock in trade. I could do this in my sleep. You two go and have fun. Enjoy your time together; don't waste it on all of this."

"You're a lifesaver, Edie," Laurie said.

"Yes, mine!" Charles chimed.

"That's enough out of you. You take this girl and buy her a good lunch."

"That's our plan." Laurie raised her hand in a sun visor to look at Edie.

They had reached the corner of Main and Water. The sun always shone in every direction at that corner, thought Charles. No matter where he seemed to look, the sun hit him full force. It was Martha's Vineyard at its most picturesque—Edgartown central with the harbour twinkling on the horizon. This is why no one had bothered Jackie Onassis when she walked down the street in the seventies; they were too busy looking at the scenery.

Edie looked up at Charles, fingering her single string of pearls. "Where are you taking her?"

"She had her eyes on Atlantic but I think I have a different idea."

"You do?" Laurie looked up at him.

"I do. Let's go for a swim on Menemsha beach and then eat at The Menemsha Galley. I'm craving one of their swordfish sandwiches." Charles licked his lips at the thought.

"Oh you two are killing me! I'm heading back to work and you two are beach-bumming!" Edie laughed. "Have fun! Laurie, I'll call you later." Edie gave them each a kiss, turned, and walked up North Water Street on heels that would have been the end of a lesser woman. She waved in shop doors as she went.

"I love Edie." Charles smiled as he watched her go.

"What's not to love?" Laurie asked. "What's her last name?"

"I don't know. I always just assumed she didn't have one. You know, like Madonna, or Prince!"

Laurie laughed. "You're a goof." Laurie looked up at Charles but stepped back when she saw that his face had lost all traces of playfulness. "What's the matter?" She followed his gaze up North Water Street. "What do you see?"

"That man."

"Which man?" Laurie asked. "I see a lot of men."

"That young black man in the white polo shirt who just came out of Fosdick's."

"What about him?"

"That's Sam Grover."

4

"Why would Sam Grover not be locked up?" Charles sat, stewing in the passenger seat of Laurie's squad car. Heavily wooded, North Road was beautiful, but Charles didn't see it. He was looking past it—through it. The events of last night were running through his head. "How can he just be walking around free buying Fosdick's fudge?"

"I have no idea, Charles." Laurie steered the car smoothly. It was an easy drive and there were no other cars to be seen. "He was driving a BMW, so maybe he lawyered up. A good lawyer could have got him out pretty quickly. Especially if someone put up bail." Her tone betrayed the fact that she cared a lot less about Sam Grover than Charles did.

"I guess." Charles wasn't convinced. "He rolled a car. He must have been driving under the influence, don't you think? Wouldn't he be charged with reckless endangerment or DUI or destruction of property? Something?"

"He might have been. Just because he's out walking around doesn't mean he wasn't charged with something. He will still be a free man until his case goes to trial—if it actually goes to trial. He might just have to pay a fine. Who knows?"

"Well, that pisses me off." Charles huffed.

"If I had gone through what you went through last night, I would be pissed off too; however, you know as well as I do that inconveniencing fellow citizens isn't a crime." Laurie glanced at him sympathetically.

He nodded his head. "You're right," Charles said. He looked out the window, this time seeing the scenery. They drove past a red gas pump standing alone in the middle of nowhere. It distracted him and made him smile. "I love that thing. It's so cool."

"It is cool." Laurie nodded in agreement.

"I wish I knew the history behind it. I'll have to look that up later." Charles said. He stared out at Chilmark as it went past his window.

"It's a real gas pump but it hasn't worked since the late 1950s." Laurie spoke without taking her eyes off the road. "Pat and Joan Jenkinson own it. Pat repainted it not too long ago. That's why it looks so good. It used to be in front of a diner that was run by Fannie and Walter Jenkinson. The gas pump was put in as a convenience for school bus drivers, mostly. I'm sure some of their fishermen friends used it too—the ones who knew where the key was hidden, anyway. When Walter died, the diner was shut down and hauled away. The family still lives just up from where the diner was. If the Jenkinsons charged a nickel every time someone stopped and took a picture of their gas pump, they'd be rich."

"Wow! I'm impressed!" Charles stared at her in awe.

Laurie shrugged. "I live here," she said matter-of-factly.

"Still," Charles said. "You're right about the pictures though. My dad and I took our picture with it back in the seventies. The paint job explains why it looks better than I remember. Brad and I took our picture with it just the other day too. I guess I owe the Jenkinsons a dime."

They drove on North Road as it wound its way through Chilmark, crossed the Menemsha Crossroad, and ended at the southeast corner of Menemsha Harbour. Laurie parked the car where the road ended, in front of the Menemsha Galley restaurant.

Charles got out of the car, stood, and stretched. Without looking to Laurie, he walked past the greyed cedar shingle building that was the restaurant and down the small beach that slipped into the harbour beside it. The back of the restaurant was a closed-in porch where you could sit and eat somewhat protected from the elements. There was a pass-through window directly from the kitchen. Charles stood beside the deck. Large posts had been driven into the ocean bed to support its structure. They were barnacled and weathered. The colour changed from brown to green to grey, marking where the water level changed with the tide. Menemsha Harbour was still very much a commercial harbour as it had been for generations. Fishermen since the early 1600s had fished there. Many of the same families still worked from the same slips. Charles looked out at the boats that were in the harbour now, lobster boats mostly, and a few draggers.

Charles heard Laurie's footsteps on the gravel coming up behind him. "Where would they have taken Sam last night?" Seeing Sam Grover on North Water Street had left Charles with his teeth clenched. He was a dog with a bone and he wasn't letting go.

"Well, I don't know how badly he was hurt, but probably Martha's Vineyard Hospital first to be checked out. From what you told me, I doubt he was in the hospital for very long, just long enough to get a nurse to bandage his head and a doctor to give him a clean bill of health. We can't have anyone suing the town of Oak Bluffs now can we?" She grinned. "Then, he would have gone to the Oak Bluffs police station." Laurie retraced her steps. She walked around the police cruiser and opened the trunk. She pulled out a multi-coloured beach bag and then closed the trunk a little harder than necessary.

"That's what I figured." Charles walked over to the cruiser and the two of them started their walk around the harbour toward Menemsha beach. "You carry a full beach bag in your trunk?"

"Always." Laurie smiled at him. "You just never know, do you?"

The sun was high in the sky now. Charles figured it must be around one o'clock. He would probably be hungry if they hadn't sampled all that cake. Laurie would be getting hungry very soon regardless of how much cake she ate. She had the metabolism of a hummingbird. He dreaded the pounds he was going to have to fight off spending time with her.

They walked back up North Road, retracing the route they had just driven. At Basin Road they turned left and headed toward the beach. On the corner was a store, Menemsha Blues. A small grey-shingled building, it looked barely large enough to house anything. Waving in front was an American flag that looked large enough to pull the whole structure over in a strong wind. There was a white van parked in front with deep blue writing and the Menemsha Blues symbol, a bluefish, painted on the side. "I've never been in there." Charles said offhandedly.

"They have some good stuff." Laurie said. "They've really taken off. They have a store on the mainland now too."

"Where?"

"Portsmouth, I think."

"Good for them. I like it when the small businessman makes a go of it. I think it's cool."

"Yeah, me too." Laurie said.

When they passed The Bite seafood restaurant, Basin Road took a turn and headed back down the hill toward the ocean. They walked passed the Menemsha Blues Charters and the Menemsha Fish Market. The harbour sparkled on their left. The water rippled in the light afternoon breeze, lit up, prepared for a postcard. As the harbour opened up, it became more industrial. Large, rusty metal draggers rested at their metal docks with greasy metal lifts. Not the postcard picture that the harbour interior portrayed at all. Transversely, on their right, in an open field of sea grass and dunes, was Jay Lagemann's well-photographed sculpture of the swordfish harpooner. After passing Larsen's Fish Market, the road opened into a small parking lot and Menemsha Beach stretched out in front of them.

Menemsha Beach was a perfect swimming beach. It was long, wide, and it didn't get as rough as South Beach. Unlike the beach in Oak Bluffs, Menemsha Beach was backed by grass and a rolling hillside. Charles remembered seeing it on a list of "Best Beaches for Living the Dream." Wedged in among the beaches of Samoa, Viet Nam, Turks and Caicos, and Australia, Menemsha Beach was heralded as the best beach in the United States. Charles couldn't argue. He could sit and stare out across the Menemsha Bight toward the Elizabeth Islands forever.

"Thank God there aren't too many people here." Laurie set down the beach bag and pulled out her bathing suit and a towel. She passed the towel to Charles. "Here, hold this up."

"Why?" Charles asked.

"Because I have to get changed!" Laurie exclaimed.

"Oh! Sorry." Charles held up the towel and Laurie stripped quickly and pulled on her one-piece, navy blue bathing suit. She folded her clothes and put them into the bag. Then she pulled out a pair of shorts for Charles and handed him a towel. She headed toward the water.

"Hey! Aren't you going to hold up the towel for me?" he asked.

"You're a guy!" Laurie called out behind her.

Charles shrugged, stripped off his clothes, and left them in a pile on the sand. Pulling on the black Under Armour shorts that Laurie had produced from the beach bag, he ran down the beach to catch up with her. The sand started warm but cooled as it dampened, as he got closer to the ocean. Charles hit the water
50

running and dove in quickly. His hands were outstretched in front of him and they sliced through the water with purpose. Charles could feel bubbles of air being pulled across his face and torso as they fought their way to the surface. He swam blind underwater. He didn't like getting salt water in his eyes. It always stung; it left them red and swollen. This way the water was only cold and fresh. Not uncomfortable but exhilarating. Swimming in the ocean made him feel alive like nothing else did. That sensation of having every inch of his body flooded with cold, clean seawater was singular. The ocean was purging, detoxifying. It wasn't an assault like chlorinated pool water. Pool water brought the body temperature down on a hot day but the other senses were left sickly and chemical ridden. In the ocean, being submerged was cleansing. All of the stresses and soils of life and living were forced from his body as he pulled himself through the waves in a broad breaststroke. Pressed together into a shallow cup, his fingers pushed the water behind him and he lurched forward. He stayed underwater until his lungs burned for air, until he had no choice. Face-first, he exploded through the ocean's surface with a dramatic gasp. Charles felt the sun kiss him immediately. How could someone not like swimming, he wondered. He opened his eyes and looked for Laurie. She was swimming closer to shore. Her hair was wet and looked darker than usual. She swam quietly in a breaststroke, moving parallel to the beach. Charles imagined that to an observer, Laurie would seem a more cautious swimmer than Charles. It was probably true. She was less exuberant, less excited. Laurie stayed above water where she had better vision, whereas Charles swam submerged and blind. His lack of caution came from growing up around water. Charles was an extremely strong swimmer. He could swim for miles. Growing up on the lakes of Ontario's cottage country, it was considered important to learn how to swim before learning to walk. It would be inexcusable to have children who couldn't swim on a lake. His entire family were excellent swimmers. Charles turned from Laurie and looked out to sea. The ocean was crystal blue. It shifted and turned, winking with sun at every movement. There were two boats on the horizon. It was impossible to tell if they were headed in or not. They were too far out. If his eyes were six inches above the water then the horizon was about sixteen hundred metres away, less than a nautical mile. Charles marvelled at the goings on between him and the boats. All the sea life that was hidden under the surface but still going about its business. Lobster, schools of fish, sharks, seals, they were all out there. Yet the ocean wasn't giving them up. "The ocean is a desert with its life underground and a perfect disguise up above." That's what America had sung in "Horse with No Name," and they had been right.

"Hey!" Laurie yelled. She was about fifty feet closer to shore than he was. "I'm hungry!"

Charles turned and looked in her direction. They had only been swimming for about a quarter of an hour. "Of course you are," Charles chuckled too quietly for her to hear before yelling out, "I'm coming!" He broke into a front crawl and headed to the beach. By the time he waded out of the ocean, Laurie was walking toward him holding out a towel. He took it and began drying his back. Laurie dried her hair.

"C'mon, hold up my towel for me." Laurie motioned over to the beach bag.

"Laurie, there's no one here."

"Just hold it."

Charles held up the towel and Laurie removed her bathing suit in front of the grassy dunes that backed Menemsha Beach. "I was thinking..."

"Yes?" Laurie asked while pulling on her jeans.

"After lunch, let's go see Jeff." Charles was looking over her, past the dunes, and into the Menemsha Hills. He didn't notice when Laurie had finished changing. She took the towel from him, jarring him back into focus.

"Jeff? Oh, *Jeff.*" She realised what he was after. She laughed. "Want to catch up with our dear friend, do you?" Laurie rolled her eyes. "You're so transparent; you want to go and grill him about Sam Grover!"

Charles shrugged. His wet bathing suit peeled from his skin as he pulled it off. "Why not? Aren't you curious?"

Laurie traded Charles his dry clothes for his bathing suit and towel. She then rolled the bathing suit into the towel and stuffed them into the beach bag. "Remind me to wash these when I go home. I don't want them to mildew."

"Aren't you?"

"Aren't I what?"

"Aren't you curious about Sam Grover?"

"Yes. I am. After we eat, we'll grab a couple of coffees at The Black Dog and take one to Jeff. Don't get your hopes up, though. There might not be a whole lot to say."

"I know. I'm just curious."

Laurie picked up the bag and started toward the harbour. "You still getting the swordfish sandwich?"

"Yep, with fresh-cut fries. You?" Charles took her hand.

"Either fish and chips or lobster roll and chips. I'll decide when I get there."

5

"I don't care whose trucks they are, Sergeant. Move them!" Charles and Laurie walked into the Oak Bluffs police station and found the room filled with the presence of a small black woman. She was standing at the desk and her eyes barely cleared the Formica counter but there was no mistake, she was there and she was commanding attention. Some people were just like that, thought Charles. There were three-hundred pound men who stood six feet, four inches tall and nobody noticed them while, conversely, there were women who barely cleared five feet and filled the room to capacity.

"They're blocking my house and I do not pay these island taxes to stare at the side of a truck while I have my afternoon tea!" The woman was wearing a tan trench coat and there was a black purse hanging over her left forearm. She wore black sensible shoes. Curls of black and grey hair wisped out from underneath a black pillbox hat decorated with violets. The violets looked real to Charles.

When the door shut behind Laurie and Charles, the old woman and the desk sergeant turned to look at them. The sergeant looked beleaguered. The woman looked over Charles with the eyes of a cat and dismissed him immediately, but she took one look at Laurie and Charles could see there was no letting go.

"You!" The woman pointed a bony finger at Laurie.

"Yes, Violet?" Laurie looked less than impressed. She sounded it too. "Please don't point your finger at me. If you have something to say, let's discuss it calmly, shall we?"

"Don't take that uppity tone with me, Chief Knickles. You're not even an islander. So many of you young people coming in these days, none of you are islanders. It's such a bother." She glared at Charles and spat her words like they were covered with vinegar.

"New blood has to come from somewhere, Violet. We can't have islanders being born with six toes, now can we?" Laurie smirked, unfazed by the old woman's dramatics. "So what's bothering you now?"

"Watch it, Chief Knickles! I will bring your actions up in front of the committee!"

56

"Mrs Beacham, I'm sure we can sort this out between us." Laurie did her best not to sound condescending. "However, if you feel the need to take it to the board, there is nothing I can do to stop you. Now what can we do for you?"

Violet pursed her lips. She looked like she was going to explode. Her words hissed out of her like the warnings of a venomous snake.

"As I was telling Sergeant Rutabaga here, there are moving trucks parked in front of my house. They're blocking my view. I do not pay taxes to stare at moving vans from America while I have my tea. I will be having my tea at precisely four p.m. this afternoon and those mainlanders had better have them moved by then!"

It always amused Charles that islanders referred to the mainland as "America"; however, he did his best to conceal it. He didn't think that Violet Beacham would see the humour.

"So, is it actually the fact that they are mainland trucks that's bothering you? If they were an islander's trucks, you would be likely to give more leeway? I know how you think islanders should be there to support each other. Especially in the face of all of these interlopers." Laurie smiled.

Violet eyed her suspiciously. "Yes—that's true. They aren't island trucks though! I saw the company name clear as the nose on my face!"

"Well, the company might very well be an American moving company, but the clients are islanders just as hoity-toity as you are. I may be the Chief in Edgartown but I do happen to know that Craig Phillips and his wife Cynthia rented the trucks. They sold their Florida rental property and they are in the process of moving some of the furniture back to the Vineyard. Craig's family has been here for a couple of generations at least and Cynthia's family is one of the original Vineyard families, are they not? At any rate, Craig sits on the board with you; maybe you can bring it up to him directly on Tuesday. I'm sure he'd love to hear from you." Laurie's voice stayed calm and her smile never wavered. Laurie had fired and Violet had taken a direct hit. They both knew it. Everyone in the room knew it. There wasn't a sound in the room. Not a breath could be heard. It seemed as if all of the traffic outside had stopped.

"Good day, Chief Knickles." Violet stormed out of the police station and did not look back. When the door closed behind her, all of the officers in the room applauded and cheered. Laurie took a bow.

"Thank you, thank you. I'm sure you all have something more important to do than stroke my ego— better get back to it. Sergeant, where's Chief Jefferies?" Laurie asked the desk sergeant who was now beaming with new life.

"He stepped out for a minute. He shouldn't be long. You and Mr Williams can wait in his office if you like." The sergeant motioned toward the office with his pen.

"Thanks. We'll do that."

Laurie and Charles walked the white-walled corridor. Not much had changed since Jeff had shown it off with pride the last time Charles had been on the island. There were new photos on the bulletin board, pictures of the Martha's Vineyard Sharks, the collegiate summer baseball team, and photos from the Oak Bluffs Library Mini-Golf Fundraiser. Someone had cut an article out of the paper noting the fundraiser had been a success. Charles grinned at the photo of Jeff putting through the mystery section. "That looks like fun. Good idea."

"It was fun, and it was a good idea. The island works hard at finding things to do on the off-season. It can get pretty drab if you don't put some effort into it. It's a real problem with our teens."

"Really?" Charles hadn't considered this prospect.

"Yes. Bored kids drink and do drugs. We try to keep them active. Still, some slip through the cracks."

"I would never have thought." Charles was stricken. Martha's Vineyard was his paradise. The thought of someone being so unhappy in a place like this that they needed to turn to drugs really upset him.

"Our addiction rate is six times the national average. Now, keep in mind that's because our population is so low. One kid really brings down the curve. Certainly more than one kid would in say, Boston." Laurie looked grim. "Still looks bad on paper, though."

"I can't imagine someone needing drugs here. The beaches, the parks, the sunsets, the ocean..."

"It all gets old pretty quick if you grew up here."

"I suppose..." Charles looked at the happy faces in the pictures of the baseball team and the fundraiser.

Laurie raised a finger and pointed at a balding man putting a ball through a stack of Harlequin romances. "That's Craig Phillips. The one I sent Violet to see. He's a good guy. I like him a lot. Everyone does."

"Who *was* that woman?" Charles exclaimed. "She was a bit much!" He followed Laurie into Jeff's office and sat down in one of the two chairs facing the chief's desk. Laurie sat beside him.

"Hmm—not the words that I would have used. Violet Beacham. She's on the Board of Selectmen in Oak Bluffs. Surprises me really. No one likes her but she's from an old Martha's Vineyard family and she's a bully. I'm not sure if that means that she bullied her way onto the board or that people think that she gets things done because she's a bully. There's probably a certain amount of truth to both. Anyway, she thinks everything is her business. I'm surprised that she

60

didn't know that those moving trucks were Craig's. She never would have come in here with both barrels blazing if she'd known that. Craig's on the Board of Selectmen too *and*, more importantly in the eyes of people like Violet Beacham, from a family even older than her own."

"So that really does matter?" Charles grinned in disbelief.

"Oh, absolutely. In their world it does. Craig would never waste his time on that crap, but a few choice words from his wife, Cynthia, and Violet could find herself blackballed from every women's auxiliary and island committee faster than you can sing 'Ladies Who Lunch'!"

Charles began to sing. "Here's to the ladies who lunch..."

"Everybody laugh." Laurie finished the Sondheim quote and then continued with her take on island politics. "I know Cynthia and I don't think that she would ever be vindictive, but I'm willing to bet that Violet Beacham isn't willing to take that chance. You know what it's like, people who *are* vindictive have difficulty believing that other people aren't."

"True story."

Jeff walked into his office carrying a coffee and a small paper bag. He was sporting a little more grey around the temples but other than that, he was the same Jeff that Charles remembered—tall and lanky.

"Hey! They didn't tell me you guys were back here!" Jeff exclaimed. "How's it going? Are you excited about the big day? It's not long now. Chris and I got our suits all ready to go!"

Charles stood to greet his friend. "They don't match, do they?"

Jeff laughed. "No. Don't be an ass."

"Good. I'm not sure I could have handled that."

"You just missed Violet Beacham." Laurie smiled wickedly.

"Oh Jeezus! I couldn't have handled *that!*" Jeff set his bag and coffee down on his desk and sat down in his chair. "What was she doing back here?"

"She had a bee in her bonnet about some trucks parked in front of her house. You know, the trucks the Phillips are using to bring their stuff back from the Florida house?"

"Yep. I saw them get off the ferry this morning." Jeff nodded in agreement and pulled an apple fritter out of the paper bag.

"Well, once I explained to her that it was the Phillips' truck, she left in a hurry." Laurie chuckled. She reached over and pulled off a piece of fritter.

"I bet she did." Jeff shook his head. "Crazy woman."

"Why was she here before?" Laurie asked.

Jeff looked at Laurie quizzically.

"You said 'back here', 'what was she doing *back here*'. Why was she here the first time around?"

"Oh. Bailing out her grandson."

"Who's her grandson?"

"Sam Grover. The guy Charles ran into last night." Jeff sipped his coffee.

"Oh Jeezus is right! No wonder she was in such a mood. She's going to be a thorn in your side until he's cleared of all charges!" Laurie said.

"That's almost exactly what she said to me this morning. I thought I was going to have to call an ambulance."

"You did?" Laurie's eyes bulged in their sockets.

"You should have seen her Laurie! When I got here this morning, I thought she was going to rip Jack's face off! Actually, what I really thought was that she was going to have a heart attack. I thought I was going to end up calling the hospital because she was going to have a stroke! I've never seen a person so worked up. Anyway, she left and took her grandson with her. Good riddance."

"What did you charge him with?" Laurie asked. She reached forward for another piece of doughnut.

Jeff snatched his fritter away. "Get your own doughnut!" He shook his head. "Grover was charged with operating under the influence, improper operation of a motor vehicle, and leaving the scene of an accident after damaging property."

"Leaving the scene, nice touch." Laurie grinned.

Charles looked at them, puzzled.

"It's the throwaway. We won't get it. We'll look like we're being nice when we cut the charges by pitching that one and getting him on the others. Which is what we wanted in the first place." Jeff explained.

"Nice."

"Was he drunk? You didn't say that he seemed drunk." Laurie looked at Charles.

"I didn't think he was drunk. I didn't smell anything either."

Jeff shook his head. "No. He wasn't drunk. He was high on coke."

"Are you sure?" Laurie asked.

"Pretty sure."

"I thought he was wired with adrenaline from the crash." Charles said.

"So did I at first, but we found some paraphernalia in the car: a mirror, a small white bag, lemon juice. The hospital will have done a tox screen."

"That's awful," Charles said.

"I was just telling Charles about the drug problems on the island. He's having a tough time adjusting to it."

"Just another day in paradise," Jeff said.

"Oh God. Please don't add Phil Collins to the list of the day's traumas." Charles sat back in his chair. "So what do you do now?"

64

"Nothing. Violet bailed him out. It's up to her to get him to court," said Jeff.

"What happened to Sam Grover's parents?" Charles asked.

"Not sure. They left him with Violet not long after he was born. Rumour has it that they just didn't want Sam anymore. Both Violet and Sam have had a tough go of it. Sam acted out, got expelled from Martha's Vineyard Regional High School. He got a lot of private tutoring which didn't give him a lot of social skills. A young boy shouldn't have to spend that much time with his angry grandmother. Violet wasn't always like this either. I mean, she was never a barrel of monkeys but she wasn't the raving maniac that you saw here today. I think people mostly feel sorry for her. She lives in a big house here in Oak Bluffs all alone with Sam...and I don't think that Sam is the best company for an old woman. She probably thinks a lot of his problems are her own fault," said Jeff.

"Well, they're not. Eventually, you have to let people be themselves," Laurie said. "That's interesting about the family history. I didn't know that. It's sad."

"Hey, you guys should come over this evening. Chris would love to see you. Dinner? Six o'clock?" Jeff asked.

"Sure." Charles stood up and shook Jeff's hand. "C'mon Laurie."

"Where are we going now?" Laurie stood up.

"I want to take a look at the crash site in the light of day."

"Oh, alright. I'm up for that." Laurie led the way out of the office. "Let's get a coffee too."

"Sure, but I don't even want to *see* a goddamned apple fritter!"

6

Pondview Drive was inland and had no distinguishing geographical features that let you know you were on Martha's Vineyard; however, it was still beautiful. The foliage was thick with maple trees and pines. Dirt driveways branched off the main roads and led their travellers to houses and homes that were, for the most part, well hidden among the trees. Except for the myriad birds crowing and cawing, it was quiet with a bucolic calm. It had no specific 'Vineyard-esque' quality.

Laurie pulled into the drive of the house that Charles' friends had rented for the wedding. Putting the car in park, Laurie leaned forward so as to get a better look at the house through her windshield. "So this is it?"

"This is what?" Charles leaned forward as well, hoping to see what she saw.

"The house that took you away from *my* place, my *oceanfront* home." Laurie said.

"Oh for Christ's sake, let it go." Charles got out of the car and closed the door.

Laurie stepped out of her side of the squad car and stretched. "I probably won't." She closed her door and walked around to Charles' side.

"I know." Charles put his arm around Laurie's shoulders and led her back up toward Pondview Drive. "C'mon. It was over here." The two of them walked up the street until they came upon the first signs of skid marks. They were black, thick, and went on for quite a distance. Laurie squatted down to look at them closer while Charles followed the tracks until he eventually came upon shards of taillight, red plastic, and pieces of glass. He remembered stepping on bits of debris the night before. This is probably what it was. He kicked them into the bush. The tire marks led off the road. Charles could make out where the car had hit the ground. Where the wheel had hit, still spinning, there was now a ditch. Ferns and other plants had been uprooted and sprayed aside. Rich earth lay open and fresh, darker and damper than the ground surrounding it. The car had hit a mailbox. The base of the wood post was still in the ground but the post itself had been ripped in half not six inches from the ground. The
68

upper half of the post was lying about five feet into the woods with the grey metal mailbox still intact. Charles could see letters inside. Steadying himself on a tree, he stepped down into the woods. The earth was soft with layers of leaves and pine needles; it gave way a few inches under his weight. He took each step gingerly and reached down for the letters in the box. Once he had them, he stood up and read the envelopes. They were all addressed to the same man, Adam Haliburton. Charles stuck the letters in his back pocket and, retracing his steps, backed his way through the woods to the road. When he reached the asphalt, Laurie reached out and gave him a hand. He stepped up and brushed himself off.

"Did you find anything?" Laurie asked.

"Not really, just a couple of letters in a broken mailbox. Sam must have taken it out when he rolled into the bush. I thought we would return them. Funny, that the residents didn't collect them. Actually, now that I think about it, it's odd that they didn't come out last night what with all the kerfuffle."

"Maybe they weren't home," Laurie said.

"That would explain it," Charles agreed. He walked over to the start of the skid and walked the length again. Looking back and forth. "How long would you say this was? Sixty feet?"

"Sounds about right." Laurie watched him.

"This road is asphalt, right?" Charles asked more rhetorically than anything else.

"Yes. Looks new," Laurie said.

"I think so too." Charles furrowed his brow and scuffed at the road with his foot. "The road is asphalt, so we can estimate the drag factor at seventy-five per cent. The skid marks are sixty feet in length and they all look to be about the same length so the braking efficiency we can assign as one hundred per cent. We're only estimating anyway. For this equation we use a constant of thirty. So, thirty times sixty times seventy-five per cent times one... What is that?" Charles looked not so much at Laurie but through her.

"You're kidding, right?" Laurie raised an eyebrow and shot him a half-smile.

"Thirteen-fifty," Charles said. "What's the square root of thirteen-fifty?"

"Do I even have to be here for this conversation?" Laurie threw her arms in the air.

"Forty."

"Forty what?" Laurie's mild irritation was shining through.

"Forty miles an hour. That's how fast our car was going when it braked. Well, actually, that's the minimum speed that the car was going when Sam braked. The first length doesn't show up on the asphalt so he could have been going a little faster than that. It certainly sounded like he was going faster than that

70

last night. Then again, I was asleep...I was going a lot slower."

"Either way, it's a hell of a lot faster than the ten mile an hour speed limit on this road." Laurie said. "I can't believe you just figured that out in your head."

Charles laughed. "Neither can I. I wish my dad had been here to see it. Math was always his thing, not mine. He would have been pleased although he would have said that it took me too long."

Laurie chortled, "Fathers and sons."

"I'd love to talk to him," Charles said.

"Your dad?"

"No—Sam Grover!"

"Why? It's not really any of your business, Charles. It's not even my jurisdiction. Sam Grover, rather Violet Beacham, is likely to sue your ass for harassment!" Laurie folded her arms across her chest.

"I suppose you're right." Charles smiled at her sheepishly. "I tend to get ahead of myself."

"I've noticed." Laurie walked over and reached for his hand. "C'mon, let's take those people their mail."

"Okay." Charles took her hand and walked toward the driveway beside the ripped up mailbox.

"What's the name on the envelope?" Laurie asked.

"Adam Haliburton. Do you know him?"

Laurie shook her head. "Never heard of him. I don't know any Haliburtons."

"Me either. There's a town in Ontario called Haliburton but that's it." Charles looked over the mail for other markings. He was looking for something that might tell him a little bit more about Adam Haliburton but there was nothing. None of the envelopes even had return addresses. Charles thought that was a bit odd but certainly not unheard-of.

"Anything?" Laurie asked.

Charles shook his head. "Nothing."

They walked down the driveway toward the modest grey-shingled bungalow. Unlike the house that Charles and his friends were renting next door, the yard for this house was messy and cluttered. There were toys and partially assembled, or disassembled, jungle gyms strewn across the brown grass. A chicken coup filled the far corner of the lawn and the constant clucking and cooing of the chickens filled the property. The roof was in need of repair. The south corner was losing its shingles and had been covered with a garbage bag, presumably to stop a leak.

"Nice place." Charles said sarcastically.

"Quiet!" Laurie scolded. "They might hear you."

There were no patio stones, no walkway markers, just a worn path across the lawn. The two of them followed it up to the front door of the house. One cement step led to the front door but there was no roof over the door and no veranda beneath it. The house was very simple and plain. It almost looked unfinished.

72

"Give me the letters." Laurie stated.

Charles handed them to her knowing that it would look better if a police chief handed over their mail than some visiting mainlander who had just finished rummaging through their bushes.

Laurie knocked. They could hear heavy rock music permeating through the doors and windows. "I doubt they'll hear anything over that crap."

"Def Leppard," Charles said.

"Is it? I used to like them in high school," Laurie said.

"I remember. I never liked them. All their songs sound the same," Charles said.

Laurie nodded. "Stripper music."

"Totally."

The front door opened and Charles felt like Def Leppard had just screamed *'Pour Some Sugar On Me!'* directly at him. Instinctively, he stepped back.

"Hi, is Adam home?" Laurie asked politely.

"No. I'm sorry he's out but he won't be long. Did you want to come in and wait?" The girl with the bright smile on her face stepped back as to welcome them in.

"Oh, no. That's alright thank you. My name is Chief Laurie Knickles of the Edgartown Police Department. Do you live here ma'am?"

"No. I'm just visiting my brother- that's Adam. I'm Mandy, Mandy Haliburton."

"Oh well, Mandy I'm afraid that there was an accident on the road last night outside your brother's house and his mailbox was damaged." Laurie pointed behind her toward the road and the scene of the accident.

"An accident? Gosh when I'm out, I'm really out. Was anybody hurt?" Mandy's eyes opened wide in what seemed to be genuine concern.

"Not seriously, no." Laurie smiled. "Well, except for your brother's mailbox. It was damaged. We just found it in the woods and retrieved some of your brother's mail from inside. I just thought we'd bring it to you."

"Thanks very much! That's nice of you." Mandy looked at Charles. "Are you a cop too?"

"No. Actually, I'm your neighbour. I'm renting the house next door with some friends. We were at the accident last night," Charles said.

"You and your friends were all out there? Wow, and I slept through the whole mess." Mandy shrugged. "Isn't that something?"

There was an awkward pause. "Yes, that's really something." Charles and Laurie said in unison. "Well, tell your brother that if he has any questions, he can call the Oak Bluffs Police Station at any time."

"I thought you was with Edgartown?" Mandy Haliburton's eyes narrowed slightly.

"That's right, I am but you should call them with your concerns. It's their jurisdiction. Enjoy your day Ms Haliburton. Bye for now." Laurie nodded her head slightly and stepped back before turning around. Charles followed suit.

"Oh, okay! Thanks for the letters! Bye!" Mandy said as they turned to leave. She stepped back inside and closed the door behind her.

Charles and Laurie marched up the slow but steady incline of the Haliburton property toward the road. The day was still warm and sunny. Light flickered the ground in a consistent current of green and yellow. The ebb and tide of the wind through maple leaves filtered the silence.

"Where to now?" Laurie looked up at Charles.

"Well, actually I think you and I are going to part-company for a bit. Is that okay? I'm going to go in the house here, have a shower, and hang out with Brooke and Brad and the gang for a while. They did come a long way to see me after all."

"That's true." Laurie smiled and then kissed him. "Go on. You could use a shower anyway. I'm going to go home for a bit and then maybe pop into the office. I might stop by and see Edie. You never know..."

"Alright. Do you want to pick me up here at six o'clock to go to Jeff and Chris's house?" When they reached the squad car, Charles put his hands on Laurie's waist and kissed her. The warm pressing of their lips made them both smile. Charles let go of her and started walking backwards, not wanting to take his eyes off of her.

"Sounds good—six o'clock." Laurie smiled and waved. She opened her car door, slipped behind the wheel, and closed the door again behind her.

Charles stopped walking and waited. There was quiet before the squad car motor turned over and revved under the hood. Charles watched as Laurie slowly backed out of the drive. The gravel sounded like popcorn as it was pressed under the tires. Laurie beeped the horn and Charles waved. All he could see was the reflection of the trees on the sun-buttered windshield but he waved anyway. In a moment, the car was gone. Charles realised that he was smiling. "That's some woman I've got there," he said.

7

Charles walked into the house to find Jamie Ross lying on the couch. Jamie hadn't moved from the couch since they got to the Vineyard. It really wasn't up to Charles to pass judgement but he had to admit that he found it a little irritating. Why come to the Vineyard if all you were going to do was watch TV? If you did only want to watch TV, wouldn't you rather do it at home? Wouldn't that be more comfortable than a rented house on a rented couch? Charles stared at Jamie stretched out on the couch in boxer shorts and a t-shirt watching America's Funniest Home Videos; he had to admit, Jamie looked pretty comfortable. Charles' trip to the Vineyard was exactly that- it was a trip *to* the Vineyard. Perhaps for Jamie it wasn't so much a trip to somewhere but rather a trip away from somewhere else. Martha's Vineyard might be Jamie's escape not his destination. What is it they say? A change is as good as a break? One of Charles' favourite quotes was, 'sometimes you have to look hard at a person and realise that they're doing the best they can. They're just trying to find their way'. It was a good quote. Charles couldn't remember who wrote it but Katharine Hepburn had said it as Ethel Thayer had in *On Golden Pond*—good movie.

"Hey!" Charles greeted Jamie.

"Hey man." Jamie offered without looking away from the television. "What did you get up to?"

"Laurie and I had breakfast at The Black Dog, took care of some wedding plans in Edgartown, we went for a swim and lunch in Menemsha, and then we came back here."

"Damn, that's too much for me. Lunch sounds good though. What did you have?" His words slurred lazily into one big word, *'waadjuav'*? Still Jamie didn't look away from the television.

"It was good. I had a swordfish sandwich and Laurie had a lobster roll at The Menemsha Galley. Kevin and Brad introduced me to that place. Are they around?" Charles was eager to have a conversation with someone else. Jamie was a good enough guy but it would be a little more interesting to have a conversation with someone who would at least make eye contact.

78

Jamie shrugged. "I dunno man."

"Ok. I'll look around," Charles said. That's what he said. What he wanted to say was, *how the hell can you not know who's in this house? You haven't left the couch in three days!* ...But he didn't.

Charles undid his laces and pulled his shoes off. He set them down neatly on the doormat and made his way through the dimly lit living room, the kitchen, and then out onto the back deck. Kevin, Brooke, and Brad were sitting on green plastic chairs, each of them nursing a beer.

"So, when are we going to meet these boys of yours?" Kevin asked Brooke.

"Oh, I'd so love to bring them here. They'd think it was brilliant! Especially Mark. Mark would love it here. He'd love the ladies! They're just his type! You see that black-haired waitress at Nancy's? He'd love her, just a wee thing with big knockers." Brooke laughed and took a sip of beer. They all looked up when Charles closed the sliding screen door with a soft rumble and a clack. Brooke leapt up from her chair, wobbled a little, and then lunged at Charles. "Oi! Hi love!" Brooke planted a big kiss on Charles and gave him a hug. "How was your morning? Are you getting the wedding sorted?" Brooke was using Charles to steady herself a little bit more than a woman did if she was on her first beer.

Charles laughed. "Liquid lunch for you today, is it?"

Brooke giggled. "Don't be cross, love. I'm on vacation now."

"I'm not cross. You go ahead and have as many liquid lunches as you see fit." Charles smiled at his friend and brushed her curly bangs out of her face. He looked over at the guys who were still in their plastic Adirondack chairs. "Hey guys."

"Hey man," they said in unison.

"Everything turn out alright at breakfast?" Brad asked.

"Absolutely. Thanks for that. Laurie thanks you too." Charles sat down in a vacant chair between the two men and Brooke sat in his lap.

Brad lifted his beer bottle in salute. "No problem. Glad it all worked out." Brad dug his hand into a Coleman cooler on the deck beside him and pulled out a Sam Adams. He passed it to Charles.

"We went out to Menemsha for a swim and had some lunch too," Charles said taking the beer.

"Where'd you go? The Galley?" Kevin asked.

"You know it," Charles said.

"Man, I love that place. Their fish is fantastic. It's so fresh. Larsen's is good too. I love fresh fish. I was out fishing this morning," Kevin said. He was always smiling. His stubbly beard was speckled grey and it framed a permanent, wide smile. His cheeks were red and his eyes sparkled. Charles figured that in twenty more years, Kevin would make a great Santa Claus.

"You were?" Charles asked incredulously.

"Oh yeah. If I'm out here on the island, I'll go every morning. There's some great fishing in the early hours. Caught some great blues. You eat fish, right?"

Charles took a mouthful of beer and swallowed before answering. "Absolutely."

"What am I saying, you're a Canadian! Of course you eat fish!" Kevin grabbed Charles by the shoulder boisterously and shook him.

Charles laughed.

"Man, I love Canada. It's a wicked place!"

"How often do you get up to Canada?"

"At least a couple of times a year. Oh yeah. I take the family up to Quebec for a fishing trip. It's wicked. There's so much to do up there. We go to Montreal too. It's beautiful up there, absolutely beautiful. I'd move to Canada in a heartbeat." Kevin stared into the sky with the expression of a man who was remembering losing his virginity to the prom queen.

Charles chuckled at his friend's almost child-like expression of his feelings. It was refreshing and endearing. Charles liked Kevin a lot. "So why don't you move there? We'd love to have you."

Kevin's face didn't stop smiling but it lost a little of its enthusiasm. "Ah, I've got a good job, so does the wife, the kids are in school…you know." Kevin shrugged.

"I get it." Charles smiled reassuringly at his friend.

Brooke got up from Charles' lap. "I've got to have a wee!"

"Well, don't do it on my lap!"

"Oi! Some blokes would pay extra for that!" Brooke winked at him and toddled off to the bathroom. She slid the screen door open with the familiar thwap that makes every North American think of summer. "Can I bring anyone anything?"

Brad stood up. "Actually, I'm going to reload with Sam Adams." Brad leaned over and swished his hand through the water that had accumulated in the bottom of the cooler. "I'm going to need some ice too."

"Grab those Doritos that are on the fridge too, would you Brad?" Kevin asked.

"Sure thing."

Charles sat back in his chair. Summer on Martha's Vineyard was an amazing thing. He wanted life to go on like this forever—maybe it would. It wouldn't be long before he had moved to the Vineyard. The paperwork was in process. How long could it take? He remembered that his friend Alex, a graphic designer, had waited for years, or so it had seemed, before he got into the States; however, he hadn't been marrying a police chief. That might speed up the process. Then,

82

Martha's Vineyard would be a full-time reality. Walks on South Beach at midnight, drinks at the Sand Bar in Oak Bluffs, morning coffees by the Edgartown Lighthouse after breakfasts at The Edgartown Inn—it doesn't get much better than that. The only thing that could possibly be better would be barbeques on Laurie's back deck on East Chop. Charles saw glasses of Kim Crawford Sauvignon Blanc, the waves washing the beach, and Laurie sitting and laughing in her Lululemon yoga pants. When that became his daily routine, Charles would have a smile on his face that would give Kevin's smile a run for its money.

*   *   *

Charles stepped out of the shower in his ensuite bathroom a lot calmer than when he had woken that morning. He dried himself off with the JAWS beach towel that he had brought with him from Toronto. Satisfied that he was dry enough to get dressed, Charles threw the wet towel over the shower bar to dry and walked into the bedroom that he shared with Brad. The white Oxford shirt and the navy blue shorts that he had ironed for dinner were hanging over the top drawer of his dresser. Charles' dresser was at the foot of his bed; Brad's dresser was across the room under the window. Brooke's room was downstairs, as was Kevin's. Charles wasn't sure where Jamie was staying; he'd never seen him get off the couch. Charles slipped his left arm into the freshly pressed sleeve of the Oxford and then his right. The afternoon had been wonderful, he thought. Charles had enjoyed a few beers but had stopped in time to sober up for supper. It wouldn't do to have him falling face first into his meal, whatever that meal may be... Charles had no idea what they were serving. He always liked to know ahead of time although he knew it was considered rude to ask. He speculated on the options while he finished dressing.

Charles walked down the stairs from the second floor to the living room. The same stairs that he had run down in the middle of the night to find out the severity of the car crash that had shocked him out of sleep. He had run out and met Sam Grover coming out of the darkness. The whole experience still didn't sit right with him. Laurie was right though, it was no business of his and he was probably going to have to leave it alone. Still, why would someone be going that fast on such a small street that didn't even lead anywhere? And then feel a need to lie about it? There was the cocaine paraphernalia to consider. Maybe that was the extent of it; maybe he was just strung out. Oh well, Charles was going to have to let it go.

Charles walked through the living room, past Jamie on the couch, and out to the back deck where he could hear laughter. He was surprised to find Laurie sitting on the deck in one of the plastic Adirondacks with the rest of the gang.

"Hey! You're early!" Charles walked over and kissed her. Laurie turned her face up to meet his kiss.

"I was ready early so I thought, what the hell?" Laurie picked up the glass of ice water that was on the arm of her chair and took a sip. She slipped an ice cube into her mouth and began to crunch on it.

"And we're glad she did!" Brooke said. "She's lovely, Charles, just lovely."

"Meh, she'll do," Charles said dryly.

Brooke hit him across the chest. Scolding him playfully. "Now, don't you start up, ya tosser! She's lovely and you treat her like she's lovely."

"Don't worry, Brooke, I'm used to it already." Laurie stood up and Charles realised that she was wearing a sundress. Charles couldn't remember the last time he had seen her in a dress. It was loose, white cotton with white embroidery across the bodice. She looked fresh and beautiful.

"Wow! You're wearing a dress!" Charles exclaimed.

"I'm wearing a dress. Yes, I'm a girl. We do things like that." Laurie looked down and straightened out her skirt self-consciously.

"I can't remember the last time I saw you in a dress!"

"Yeah, well don't make a big deal about it or you may never see me in one again." Laurie walked past him toward the screen door. "C'mon let's get going."

"You look beautiful," Charles said.

"Would you shut up?" Laurie's face flushed. "C'mon, we're going to be late."

"Alright, let's go." Charles turned to his friends. "Good night everyone. Have fun!"

"We will. Have a lovely night, my dears." Brooke kissed him and then walked over and kissed Laurie as well. "It was so lovely to sit and have a chat with you, Laurie. We'll see you again before the wedding, right?"

"Absolutely," Laurie said.

Charles and Laurie walked through the living room, past Jamie on the couch, and out the front door. Once the door was closed, Laurie turned to Charles. "What's with the guy on the couch?"

Charles laughed. "I have no idea. I swear I'm going to leave this island with a wedding ring and a mug from The Black Dog. Jamie's not going to leave with anything but bed sores."

"Weird," Laurie said.

"I know," said Charles.

"Why do you want a mug from The Black Dog?"

"I think they're cool," said Charles.

"If you say so."

They got into the squad car and headed down Pondview Drive to Barnes Road. The summer sun was getting lower but it was nowhere near dark. As they drove into the heart of Oak Bluffs, Charles could see hints of Lagoon Pond sparkling through the trees on their left. On the right, they passed occasional dirt roads and drives. Otherwise, Barnes Road was heavily wooded. Property here was less expensive because it wasn't on the ocean but it was just as pretty. There were some beautiful inland homes on the Vineyard.

"How was your afternoon?" Charles asked somewhat absently. He remembered reading that most people couldn't handle more than four minutes of silence before they had to make conversation. Charles wondered how long that had been.

"It was good. I went home and had a quick shower and then I ended up having a nap, actually. I didn't go into the office at all. I called but there was nothing really going on so I figured, the hell with it." Laurie spoke brightly.

"Sounds good. I spent my afternoon on the deck, chatting. They're a good bunch."

"They seem like it. I really enjoyed them." Laurie turned and smiled at him broadly. They both jumped when her iPhone rang. She reached into her small white purse, pulled it out, and answered it. "Hello? ...We're on our way... Charles is here with me...*Gay Head? Now?* ...Alright, we'll be there in fifteen minutes." Laurie hung up and placed her phone back in her purse. "That was Jeff."

"What did he want?"

"He wants us to meet him by the Gay Head Lighthouse!"

"What about dinner?"

"Charles you heard the conversation," she snapped. They were silent for a moment. Laurie's face flushed. "I'm sorry, I didn't ask." Laurie turned the cruiser onto a driveway, pulled back into a three-point turn, and started driving back the way they came. Now with Lagoon Pond on their right, the cruiser drove past Pondview Drive at a much greater speed than it had left it. Laurie steered down Barnes Road until they came to Edgartown West Tisbury Road. They made a left, continued to State Road and followed that through Chilmark. For the most part, they drove in silence. Putting an end to the four-minute theory. Neither of them had anything to say. All either of them could think about was why their friend and potential dinner host was calling them out to the opposite end of the island so urgently when he should be opening his front door and welcoming them inside for supper. Neither one of them had any idea what Jeff wanted but they both shared the suspicion that it wasn't good news. They didn't even want to speculate. Somehow, saying anything out loud would just make everything worse. So, they drove in silence. The evening had taken a somewhat ominous tone.

As they neared the lighthouse, the trees became fewer and fewer and then disappeared. On Gay Head, the tundra was long, wind-swept grass and rock. Charles' eyes were drawn to a cluster of lights. Other than the lighthouse, there wasn't a whole lot on Gay Head. The flashing multicoloured lights stood out. Almost at the base of the lighthouse, was an assembly of police cars, ambulances, and fire trucks lining State Road. Laurie pulled up quietly behind the other squad cars. She reached into her purse and pulled out her badge. She clipped it to her dress. "What the hell is this bullshit?" she asked rhetorically. "This is not how I planned to spend my night off."

"Let's go find Jeff," Charles said, opening his car door and stepping out onto the dew-laden grass.

The two of them walked up the road. Jeff was easy to spot. He was easily four inches taller than everyone around him. When he saw them, Jeff turned toward them, eyed them up and down, and grinned a half-smile. "For what it's worth, you two look great!"

"Thanks. I feel like one of Charlie's Angels." Laurie looked past him, trying to assess the situation. "What's going on, Jeff? Why aren't we all sitting at your dining room table right now drinking copious amounts of wine?"

"Don't even talk about it. Chris is pissed off enough as it is. He's convinced that I do this to him on purpose." Jeff pointed toward the head. "We have ourselves a car accident. A car drove off State Road and over the head. We're trying to get the car and the driver up now." Jeff began to lead them toward the scene of the accident.

"Is the driver going to be alright? Is he still in the car?" Laurie asked.

"No. He was thrown from the car. We found him about thirty feet from the vehicle," Jeff said. He looked over his shoulder at Charles and Laurie. "He's dead."

"Jesus. That's too bad." Laurie looked grim. "Was he an islander?"

"I don't mean to sound insensitive," Charles interjected, "but why are we here? You're the Police Chief of Oak Bluffs and," he turned and motioned toward Laurie, "she's the Police Chief of Edgartown. I kind of see Chris's point—why are we here?"

"The Martha's Vineyard Drug Task Force is part of the Oak Bluffs Police Department and it looks like this is going to be part of an existing Oak Bluffs case— so I'm it. As for you guys," Jeff said. "I thought you might want to be here. The driver of the car was Sam Grover."

Laurie and Charles stared at Jeff in shocked silence.

"Yeah—Sam Grover is dead."

8

Not one of them spoke for what seemed like a very long time. Charles didn't know how long it was but he was sure that it was longer than four minutes. They stood facing the Gay Head cliffs, watching the rescue team hard at work, bringing up the car and the body of Sam Grover. The constant crash of the waves on the beach below sounded a haunting echo of the accident. Some tourists were watching the goings on but most of them went about their business at the pinnacle of the head, preoccupied by shopping for souvenirs and pies made by Wampanoag Indians. The sun was getting lower and they were lit more and more by the flashing of the emergency lights. Sam Grover came up zipped into a black rubber body bag. Two men carried him to an ambulance and lay him gently on a stretcher. The headlights of an approaching vehicle flitted across

Charles, Laurie, and Jeff briefly before finding the road once again. The three of them turned to face the oncoming car.

The taxi rolled up beside them and stopped. Slowly, the rear passenger door opened and a small woman stepped out. It was Violet Beacham. She was dressed in a navy coat and the same black pillbox hat that she had been wearing the first time Charles had seen her. She wore black gloves and carried her hands folded together across her chest. Her simple black purse was slung over her left forearm. If he didn't know better, he might have thought that she was there to collect for the Salvation Army. She struck Charles as having an ecclesiastic austerity. There was no doubt in Charles' mind that Violet Beacham attended church regularly.

"Chief Jefferies. Chief Knickles." Violet spoke formally without emotion. Her face was stoic.

"Mrs Beacham, thank you for coming." Jeff held out his hand and she shook it with ceremonious brevity.

"You said there had been an accident," Violet said.

"Yes ma'am. There has," Jeff said.

"Is it my Samuel?" Violet asked. Her eyes focused on the action happening behind them. Her expression was stern.

"I'm afraid it is. Mrs Beacham, I'm sorry but Sam seems to have lost control of his vehicle and driven it off the cliff. We don't have all the details yet; we're still working on getting the car up but... Mrs Beacham, Sam is dead."

"I see." Violet turned her eyes back to Jeff. "So, my grandson has succeeded in destroying both of my vehicles. Chief Jefferies, I will need a full report to submit to my insurance company. See that I get it."

Jeff stared at her incredulously. "Mrs Beacham, did you hear what I said?"

"Chief Jefferies, I may be ninety years old but my hearing is as sharp as it ever was. I'll thank you not to condescend to me." Violet turned to step back into her taxi. "I imagine that you will have some questions. Come to my house for tea tomorrow at four o'clock sharp. I will make myself available to you then. Good night Chief Jefferies, Chief Knickles." Violet pulled the taxi door closed and the car drove off into the gloaming.

"What the hell was that?" Jeff exclaimed.

"*That* was Violet Beacham," Laurie said. "No more, no less."

"Is she made of ice? Does she feel nothing? I don't think I've ever met such a hateful woman in all my life." Jeff shook his head in amazement.

Charles wasn't so sure. The woman he had seen in the police station that afternoon had been angry, very angry. The woman he had just seen had not been angry at all. This had been a very different woman. Very thick walls had been erected in self-defence. He watched Violet Beacham's taillights fading in the distance. Charles suspected that there was a lot more to Violet Beacham than she was willing to let on.

"I don't think that there's anything else that we can do here. My detectives can handle it. Let's go and get our dinner," Jeff said forcing a smile at Charles and Laurie. "I'll tell Chris we're coming."

"Thank God! I'm starving!" Laurie said. "Jeff, we'll follow you in our car."

*   *   *

Prime rib, mashed potatoes, green beans, carrots, and cauliflower, with homemade Yorkshire puddings and gravy—Charles, Jeff, and Laurie walked into a house full of rich aromas that made all of them think of Sunday dinners and holiday feasts. Chris and Jeff's house wasn't all that far from Laurie's. They lived in Harthaven. Charles had never heard of Harthaven before but when he looked it up, he found that it had been around for quite some time.

Harthaven was a community first settled by William H. Hart, a railroad man who had fallen in love with Martha's Vineyard when he first travelled there in 1857. When Hart returned in 1871, he purchased five lots of land from the township of Oak Bluffs and the

94

Wharf Company. He expanded not long after that by buying an additional three lots. The expansion continued until Harthaven began at the seawall of Oak Bluffs and continued to Sengekontacket Pond. In the beginning, the community existed solely of William H. Hart's family members but it expanded exponentially as prominent Martha's Vineyard families like the Eddys, the Youngs, the Phillips, and the Beachams for that matter, married into the Hart family. Quite of a few of the old families were still there and several of Hart's houses were still standing. Charles found the whole island history fascinating.

Dinner had been warming all night and they all sat down to eat as soon as Charles, Laurie, and Jeff got in. Jeff and Chris sat at the ends of the dining room table while Charles and Laurie sat across from each other on the longer sides. The table was covered in serving dishes full of food and covered with tin foil.

"Sorry if some of the vegetables are a little overdone but they wouldn't have been if we had sat down on time." Chris winked at Charles and Laurie but the look he gave Jeff was a little sterner.

"It couldn't be helped!" Jeff pleaded his innocence at his husband.

"I know, I know, police business," Chris said, rolling his eyes. "Doesn't mean I have to like it."

"I suppose not," Jeff looked genuinely sorry.

"Let's eat!" Chris said smiling broadly. It was clear that Chris had every intension of saving the evening.

"I'm starving!" Laurie said. She reached for the prime rib that had already been expertly carved by Chris. She helped herself to two large cuts before passing it across the table to Charles. "This looks awesome."

"Does it ever!" Charles agreed.

"So what took you out at this hour anyway?" Chris asked.

"Remember my Sam Grover story?" Jeff said.

"The guy that Charles tried to help last night?"

"That's the one," Jeff said.

"What about him?"

"He drove his car off the Gay Head cliffs."

"What? How the hell did he do that? That has to be no mean feat!" Chris exclaimed.

"No kidding." Laurie nodded passing Chris the carrots.

"We won't have all the details until we get the car up." Jeff passed the green beans to Charles.

"How's the kid?" Chris asked.

"Dead." Jeff, Charles, and Laurie all spoke the one word in unison and it hung heavily over the table for a few moments before fading away.

Finally, Chris spoke. "Jesus. That's awful."

"It really is." Laurie nodded in agreement.

96

Chris shook his head. "That poor woman."

"Who?" Jeff asked.

"Well, didn't you tell me that he was Violet Beacham's grandson? He was all she had. This is going to be really tough on her."

"You might not say that if you had seen her out on the head this evening!" Jeff scoffed.

"Why?" Chris poured gravy over everything on his plate and then scanned the table. Satisfied that everyone else had already done the same, he set the gravy boat down on the sideboard behind him.

"Her response when I told her that Sam had died was *'so my grandson has succeeded in destroying both of my automobiles'*. I kid you not."

"I don't buy it," Chris said.

"It's true. I was standing right there. Charles and I both heard it," Laurie said.

Charles sat quietly and listened.

"Oh, I believe that's what she said; however, I don't believe that's how she really feels. Violet Beacham is old school. She's not going to wear her heart on her sleeve. Like my grandma always said, *'Never let them see you ache'*," Chris said. "Mark my words, she's in a lot of pain right now...and she's all alone."

A sombre silence fell across the dining table.

"What do you think Charles?" Jeff asked.

"I agree with Chris actually." Charles' expression was empathetic.

"Really, eh?" Laurie said. "Maybe Jeff and I have become too jaded by police work."

"They haven't endured Violet Beacham screaming and bitching on a fairly regular basis either," Jeff said.

Laurie laughed. "That's true. Maybe we're not so much jaded by police work as we are by Violet Beacham herself." Laurie stood up. "I'd like to propose a toast!"

"Here's to the ladies who lunch!" Chris laughed.

"Everybody laugh! We just quoted that song this morning! That's kind of weird," Charles said.

"Can't go wrong with Sondheim." Chris nodded. "I know that it's Elaine Stritch's song but have you seen Patti Lupone sing it at Sondheim's eightieth birthday party? Amazing."

Laurie cleared her throat and glared at the two of them.

"Sorry," Charles said sheepishly. "Do go on."

"I would like to toast our hosts, Jeff and Chris. Thank you for having us. Thank you, Chris for making this fantastic meal and for your patience in serving it to us!" Laurie laughed. "To Jeff and Chris!"

"To Jeff and Chris!" Charles repeated and raised his glass. Laurie sat back down and all four of them clinked glasses.

"Alright, this food has waited long enough. Let's eat!" Chris said.

Laurie cut a piece of prime rib, scooped up a smidgen of horseradish and popped it all in her mouth. "Oh man, this is good."

9

Charles woke up early. He always woke up early. Laurie hadn't dropped him off at the house until midnight but he was awake shortly after five. Brad snored lightly in the bed across the room as Charles slipped on his shorts and T-shirt. He padded quietly down the stairs. Not five feet away from Jamie, who was passed out on the couch, Charles pulled on his Nike Shox and headed out to greet the day.

The morning was bright. The sun was still too low to be seen from his vantage point in the woods but Charles could look up and see a clear, bright blue sky framed by rich, green trees. When the last of the gravel drive had crunched beneath his feet, Charles headed north toward Barnes Road and the downtown centre of Oak Bluffs. He wouldn't be meeting Laurie for a while yet. That gave him a few hours to hike around the island by himself. He would grab a coffee at Mocha Mott's and then head along the beach towards Edgartown. It was a long hike but it wasn't the first time that he had done it. He would do it again too. Getting up early, being alone, and walking, these were three of Charles' favourite things. Combining them was sublime. There was a peace in the early morning tranquillity. There weren't many people out but the people who were out were very friendly. Everyone Charles passed on the street in the early hours waved, nodded and smiled, or offered a bright 'good morning' as they passed. It was nice. Even in the big city that was true. There was something about early morning people. He loved them.

The walk into downtown Oak Bluffs was not a complicated one. Charles followed Barnes Road which, when it crossed County Road, became Wing Road, and Wing Road eventually became Circuit Avenue. Circuit Avenue was the hub of downtown Oak Bluffs. From one end to the other it was filled with restaurants, bars, and souvenir shops. There was Sharky's Cantina, a satellite of the larger Sharky's in Edgartown, Linda Jean's restaurant, the island's omnipresent Black Dog, Mocha Mott's, and The Corner Store. Charles loved The Corner Store. It was the best place on the island to get cheap and cool souvenirs not to mention everything that you would need for a day at the beach. Across the street, there was Slip 77—the hippest shop in Oak Bluffs—sitting impressively in its new location. Circuit Avenue cut through the heart of downtown and ended at the old Island Theatre and the Flying Horses Carousel. After Circuit Avenue was Lake Avenue. On Lake Avenue, there were cool restaurants and bars like Nancy's Bar & Grill, The Sand Bar, and Lobsterville. All good reasons for visiting Oak Bluffs but all of those reasons were moot at this time of day. When Charles got into downtown it was still very early and other than Mocha Mott's, everything was closed up tight. Circuit Avenue would be a bustling hub of activity in a matter of hours but for now it was quiet. Looking around at the amount of available parking made Charles grin. That would certainly not be the case in a couple of hours.

Charles walked down the metal steps that led to the storefront of Mocha Mott's. He pulled open the generic glass and steel door and walked in. Mocha Mott's was small. There were a couple of people standing around inside. One man was talking and laughing with one of the baristas and the other reading the Vineyard Gazette. The Pretenders' *Brass In Pocket* was playing on the stereo. The room was rich with the aroma of freshly ground beans and brewed coffees. There were Mocha Mott's t-shirts, traveller mugs, and other paraphernalia pinned to the wall, displayed for sale. Charles considered buying a traveller mug briefly but decided against it.

"What can I get you, bud?" A hipster with a pleasant face and soft smile stood at the cash register across a wooden counter.

"I'll have an extra large cappuccino with- how many shots do you make that with?" Charles asked.

"Four," The barista responded.

"Okay with two extra shots of espresso please," Charles said politely.

"Six shots! Rough night last night?" The barista joked as he rang up Charles' order.

"No. I just like my coffee strong."

"I'll say. You'll be able to stand a spoon up in your cup...if the coffee doesn't eat it away first!" The barista took the money from Charles, made change, and then set about making the beverage. The Pretenders had faded into David Bowie's *The Man Who Sold The World*. Mocha Mott's was a cool spot.

Coffee in hand, Charles continued down Circuit Avenue, turned right at Lake Avenue, and followed it up around Ocean Park to Seaview Avenue. He crossed the street to the ocean side and walked south. Seaview Avenue, indeed. The sidewalk was on top of a man-made breaker wall of enormous and jagged stones. Charles estimated that he must have been looking down from about one and a half storeys. Beyond the breaker wall was the beach. Past that, the ocean went on for miles to the horizon. The sun was low, almost indistinguishable from the reflection on the ocean's surface. White light streaked down from the sky and shot across the water like a dance of lightning. Charles had to squint to look toward the spectacle and even then he could not look directly at it. Rhythmically, the morning waves rolled into shore. This beach never got rough unless it was during a storm but in the morning it was particularly calm. Gulls soared and squawked above him, curious enough to ask for food but wary enough to keep their distance. There was a parking lane on the side of the road closest to Charles but there were only three cars parked in it. Presumably, they belonged to the few people on the beach. There was a man throwing a stick for his golden retriever and two couples with traveller mugs. Charles continued his walk, his gaze almost permanently fixed on the beach and the rolling ocean. He turned occasionally to check the park but for the most part, it was the beach that held his imagination captive. There were parks to look at in Toronto but there was no ocean. He inhaled the scents deeply. The air was cool but heavy with the smell of salt and seaweed. It was fresh and unadulterated. Even though the sun was low, it was warm. Charles was only wearing a navy blue Martha's Vineyard t-shirt but it was enough.

Seaview Avenue turned as it passed the park. It then passed Lover's Rock as it entered Harthaven and became Beach Road. The houses of Oak Bluffs were behind him now and had been replaced by Farm Pond. The road was quiet. Charles hadn't imagined there would be much traffic at this time. It would be another hour at least before the business traffic started up on the island. There was a curious lack of bicycle traffic though, thought Charles. Cyclists were usually out in full force by this point—not this morning. There was no one. Still, Charles stayed on the ocean side of the street, leaving the bike path to anyone who might come along. Cyclists in Toronto could be testy about sharing bike paths with pedestrians. Charles decided that there was no need to test if that was a global attitude or not.

A red SUV roared past Charles—he jumped. His heart leapt into his throat as it raced by him. He hadn't heard it coming. That was not like Charles at all. His spatial intelligence was usually one of his strengths. He watched the truck drive into the distance. Odd, he thought. The SUV had no license plate, just a black frame where the plate should have been. Charles knew that in some special circumstances, vehicles were only issued one plate but he also knew that in those situations, the plate was to be displayed on the rear. No matter what, there should be a plate on the back of that car. The SUV disappeared around the corner. Once again, the road was quiet. Charles was alone.

Charles' heartbeat slowed and he laughed at himself for being so jumpy. The morning was perfect.

He was walking down a major roadway and a car goes by him and makes him jump. He felt fairly foolish. Charles took a mouthful of Mocha Mott's cappuccino. It was so good. Charles heard the soft rumble of another car engine in the distance. He looked up through the sunlight to see the same red SUV heading toward him.

Charles' chest tightened. He didn't like this car at all. He had no reason to feel this way. The car had driven by him once. He had jumped. So what? It had no rear license plate. Big deal. That was a police issue not his! The SUV got closer. It was moving quickly. The rumble of the engine changed pitch. It was an octave higher now. Had it sped up? It was close enough for Charles to see that there was no front license either. Charles continued walking. His heart was beating faster. His walk was as casual as he could muster. Charles wanted to run away. The SUV ignored a twist in the road like it was aiming directly for him. One hundred feet, eighty feet, it was closing fast. Sixty, fifty, forty... Charles jumped out of the way and the truck missed him by two feet. The force of the wind from the passing vehicle pushed Charles into the ground. Charles hit the pavement at his temple. The weight of his own body made his neck crack. His torso fell heavily to the ground. Charles heard himself grunt as the wind was knocked out of his lungs.

The tires on the SUV screamed behind him. Charles knew that the truck was braking. Leaving skid

106

marks like the ones Sam Grover had left. Charles pressed the palms of his hands onto the pavement to push him up. He had to get up. He heard the truck reversing. Shakily, Charles stood and turned around. The truck was about eighty feet away. The driver pushed his foot hard on the gas and the SUV leapt forward directly at Charles. Charles ran across the street toward Farm Pond. He tried to jump the guardrail but he tripped and fell onto the bike path. The skin on his hands tore away as he skidded across the asphalt. His face made a sickening *thunk* as the same temple bounced off the ground. Charles could hear the SUV screeching as it ground metal into wood, splintering along the rail, filling the space where Charles had just tripped. All Charles could hear was the roar of the truck engine. It was right on top of him. Charles rolled into a ball. His muscles tightened. His body prepared to feel the force of the entire truck landing on him. The crush of his ribs giving way under the leviathan was imminent—he was sure of it. Instead, he only felt its breath exhale across him, as it roared past. Charles staggered to his feet once more. The truck seemed to be panting, heaving like an angry bull. The truck's headlights were focussed, staring at him. The front corner was dented and scarred where it had run along the rail. The sun's reflections forbid Charles from getting any glimpse at the driver.

Charles felt sick. There was bile in his throat. Sweat glued his clothes to his torso. His knees were warm and sticky. Charles didn't have to look to know that he was bleeding. His lungs burned with every heave of his chest. He reached into the front pocket of his shorts and pulled out his iPhone. He tossed it onto a grassy hill on his right hand side. He looked over his shoulder at Farm Pond. It was smooth, green, and glossy. It looked cold—less than inviting. He looked back toward the truck. Growling meanly, it hadn't moved. Charles turned back and waded into the pond. With his first step, he sank mid-calf in muck. The water was freezing but he waded in anyway. The truck couldn't get him in the pond. If it tried to follow him, it was not getting out. As his second step sunk, Charles pulled his first foot out of the muck with a vulgar slurp. His sock foot came out wet, brown, and minus a shoe. He kept going. Charles winced as the salt water stung his fresh abrasions. Keeping his balance was a struggle. His whole body shook, fighting desperately to stay upright. He turned back to look at the road—the truck was gone. Charles looked up the road toward Oak Bluffs and down toward Edgartown; there was nothing. The road was empty. Just as empty as it had been before he was attacked. Charles turned around and sunk his shoeless foot back into the pond bed. He twisted out his second foot, again without a shoe. He grimaced. The cold worked its way up his legs and into his torso. It felt like a mallet of ice smashing into his navel, the cold shards permeating his abdomen. Pain squeezed through him as he cramped. This isn't good at all, he thought. More bile rose in his throat. Vomit rushed into his mouth and he projected it into the freshly stirred, murky pond water. Charles forced himself upright. The trees on his left bent over and became the trees on his right. There were stars in the water. Charles watched the broad strokes of sky, vomit, and mud swirl into Vincent Van Gogh's Starry Night. He fell backward into the pond. The cold water wrapped around him like a freezer bag. Charles felt every muscle in his body let go; there was nothing he could do to fight it. He felt the water pull away from his face. Charles closed his eyes.

10

Laurie was sitting in a green leather club chair when Charles woke up. She had her hair pulled back into a ponytail and the screen on her MacBook bathed her face in unnatural light. Drugstore reading glasses were propped on her nose but she still squinted as she typed. Laurie only wore her glasses when she used the computer. Charles looked around the room. He was in the hospital. Through the vertical white slats, Charles could see the Vineyard sprawling outside toward the Atlantic. "Good morning," Charles said. His voice was rough betraying a dry throat. "At least I think it's morning."

"Jesus Christ! Thank God." Laurie lifted the computer off her lap, took off her glasses, and hurried toward his bed. "What the hell happened to you?"

"How did I get here?" Charles lifted his right hand to find an intravenous taped to it.

"A couple of joggers found you." Laurie picked up a pitcher of water and poured him half a glass. "They found your phone first, actually. Why did you take your phone out of your pocket? Oh and before you ask—yes, we have your shoes too. You can thank Jack for that the next time you see him. He made a mess of himself getting the damned things out of the mud!"

"Where are they?" Charles looked around the room for them.

"At my place." Laurie managed a smile and rolled her eyes. "It must be a guy thing; I would have left them there and just got a new pair. They're probably ruining my washing machine as we speak." Laurie's face lost all humour. "Charles, what happened?"

Charles stared at her and watched her eyes get glassy. A well of tears collected on her bottom lid. He could feel his eyes doing the same thing. He couldn't believe the words that were about to come out of his mouth. He tried to chuckle but the chuckle was awkward and out of place. "Someone tried to kill me," he said. Charles felt a wave of emotion crash over him. He shuddered and choked back a full cry. He flushed with embarrassment. Charles had read about victims of head injuries experiencing powerful emotions but this was the first time he had experienced it for himself.

Laurie got up on the bed and wrapped her arms around him gently. They were quiet for a while. "Charles, are you sure?" she finally asked him.

Charles told her the story of the red SUV with no plates. He watched her expression change from worry to disbelief to horror as the story unfolded.

"But...why?" Laurie asked. "Why would someone want you dead?"

Charles shook his head. "I have no explanation." The sudden emotion of admitting that someone had tried to kill him had passed. Charles had regained his composure.

"Well, we'll check the department of motor vehicles for a red SUV—actually, how can we? It didn't have plates and there's no reason for us to assume it was local. It could be from anywhere! What kind of SUV was it?" Laurie asked.

"I don't know." Charles flushed with mild embarrassment again. "I don't know cars."

"You don't know? *With all that trivial shit you've got locked away in your head?* It had no plates *and* you don't know what make it was?" Laurie took an exasperated deep breath. Her frustration was with the situation not with Charles. "Sorry, I don't mean to yell at you. I'm just freaked out," she apologised and thought for a minute. "Is there anything that you can tell me about the car?"

"Well, the front corner is all dented in where it struck the railing. That should make it stand out. Also, it was old."

"Old? What makes you say that?" Laurie's brow was furrowed. She was dressed casually in jeans and a t-shirt but Charles could tell that he was talking to Chief Knickles.

"Well, it was in good shape. You know, clean and shiny. The paint job was good, no rust but it had corners, real corners. Cars nowadays are so rounded. The headlights too, they were square and didn't wrap around the corners." Charles thought back to the headlights glaring at him.

"What else do you remember about the headlights?"

Charles thought about it. "They were yellow on the outside."

"What colour was the grill?"

"Silver."

"How many windows down the side?" Laurie asked.

"Three. It was a four door."

"Anything you can tell me about the tires?" Laurie pushed. "Did they look normal or kind of flat?"

"Normal," Charles said. "Not like fishermen tires." Charles knew that a lot of the fishermen on the island partially deflated their tires for beach driving.

"Okay," Laurie smiled at him. "Well, the paint sample from the railing is being tested as we speak. We should have something pretty soon." She stood from the bed. "When did all of this happen?"

"Maybe six in the morning?" Charles looked for a clock. There wasn't one. "What time is it now?"

"Nine. The joggers found you around a quarter to seven," Laurie said. "You weren't out that long."

"Well, I'd like to go home now," Charles said. "Where are my clothes?"

"Whoa! Just hold on a minute there, Charles Williams. Let me see if I can track down a doctor and see what he says. You seem fine to me but I'm not a doctor."

"Big deal. A doctor's only a regular guy who's read a book," Charles said.

"Yes, well, I haven't read that book so I'm just going to go and get the doctor and see what he says. Stay put!" Laurie pointed her finger at him and gave him a look that let him know she meant business.

"Yes, Chief."

"That's better. I'm getting married on the weekend and I would really like it if you were there too." Laurie started to walk out of the room but turned back around. "You didn't tell me, why did you take your phone out of your pocket? Or did it just fall out in the commotion?"

"No, I took it out. I knew that the truck couldn't follow me into the pond but I also knew that if I got my phone wet, I would be really screwed. My plan had been to wade into the pond until the truck left and then wade back out and call you." Charles shrugged but winced; his back hurt. "It almost worked."

"It was a good idea—I'll give you that." Laurie left in search of a doctor.

Charles lay back and soaked in the scene outside his window. It was another perfect day on Martha's Vineyard. A perfect day and he was spending it in a hospital bed. This had certainly not been part of his plans when he was taking the ferry over from the main land or 'America' as the locals called it. Why in God's name would someone try to kill him? The only thing out of the ordinary that had happened to him on this trip was the Sam Grover car accident—and Charles had tried to *save* him! It hardly seemed like a punishable offense. Besides, Sam was dead now. He'd driven himself off the Gay Head cliffs. Charles hadn't had anything to do with that. Sadly, that had been Sam's own doing—all by himself. So why had someone tried to mow Charles down in broad daylight? How did they know he would be there? Had they followed him? It was a very scary feeling to think that someone had been stalking him the whole morning.

Laurie returned with a doctor in tow. He was an older man in a white lab coat. This man had no choice but to become a doctor, Charles thought. His hair was grey and he wore black horn-rimmed glasses perched on a strong nose and round cheeks. His was an intelligent and kind face, thought Charles.

"Good morning, Charles. I'm Dr Bob Nevin. You gave the police chief here quite a scare," Dr Nevin smiled. When he smiled, his eyebrows lifted reflexively. Charles' grandfather's eyebrows used to do the same thing.

"I assure you it was not intentional," Charles grinned.

"I'm sure." The doctor took out a penlight and shone it in Charles' left eye and then his right. "How are you feeling now?"

"I feel fine," Charles said.

"You've got quite a bump on your head." The doctor held up a finger. "Follow my finger, please." He moved his hand back and forth. Charles followed it easily. "You've got some good scrapes too." Dr Nevin stepped back. "Your eyes seem fine. Have you tried standing up?"

"No, not yet." Charles was a bit embarrassed that he hadn't thought to try on his own.

"Why don't you give it a try for me now, alright?"

Charles lifted the blankets and swung his legs over the side of bed. It was the first time he was getting a good look at some of the damage. His legs were badly bruised. His knees had been bandaged up tight.

116

Charles winced at the stiffness in his bruised joints as the weight of his legs forced his knees to bend. Standing was going to be a bigger challenge than Charles had previously thought. Briefly, he thought better of it. Slowly, he put his weight on his legs and lifted himself off the bed. He kept his right hand on the mattress, more for psychological reassurance than for physical support. His knees ached. His feet throbbed with the new pressure on his sore joints. Charles stepped forward with one foot and then the other. He could walk. Slowly but he could walk.

"How does that feel?" asked Dr Nevin.

"Okay." Charles tried to smile. "A bit sore but okay."

"Hmm..." said Dr Nevin. "That probably means it hurts quite a bit."

Laurie chuckled. "He's got you pegged, babe."

Dr Nevin smiled at Laurie and turned back to Charles. "Do you live alone, Charles?"

"No. I am living with a bunch of friends this week. One is quite the mother hen. Even worse than this one!" He motioned toward Laurie. She stuck out her tongue at him.

"That's true actually, Dr Nevin. I've met the woman; she won't give him a moment's peace if he goes home looking like this. When he's not at home, he'll be with me. I don't plan on letting him out of my sight."

"Well, normally I would like to keep a patient overnight for observation but you seem to have a good support system Charles. You're a lucky man." Dr Nevin smiled broadly.

Charles looked at Laurie with deep and thoughtful eyes. "I am lucky," he said.

"I'll give you a cane to use and then sign you over to Chief Knickles. If you have any blackouts or dizzy spells, I want you to come right back here. Understood?"

"Absolutely," Charles said.

"Alright. I'll go and get you that cane." Dr Nevin turned to leave but then paused. "Oh, I understand that congratulations are in order. You two are getting married this weekend!"

"We are. If he doesn't get himself killed first," Laurie said. "It's a very informal affair, Dr Nevin. We'd love it if you and Mrs Nevin would come. We didn't even send out formal invitations. We've just been asking friends to join us. I'll get Edie to get in touch with you."

"Barbara would love it. I'll talk to her this evening. Thank you very much," Dr Nevin said. "That Edie is a wonderful girl. I go to The Edgartown Inn regularly for Edie's breakfasts. I even have a regular table. That coffee cake of hers is something special."

"You don't have to tell us—we're regulars ourselves. You'll be right at home then. The wedding is taking place at The Edgartown Inn. It's a special place for us."

"Until the weekend then." Dr Nevin walked out of the room with the comfortable stride of a man who had worked in a hospital for a long time. Only hospital employees ever had that gait.

Laurie scooped up the pile of clean clothing on the dresser that she had brought with her. "Let's get you dressed," she said. She bent over and gently slid the pair of shorts over his feet and up his legs, all the while being mindful of his bruises. At the waist, Charles took them and did them up. She passed him a clean *JAWS* t-shirt. Charles lifted his arms to put it on and winced as the muscles in his back reacted to the stretch.

"That son-of-a-bitch really did a number on you," Laurie said. She shook her head in anger and disgust.

"And here I was, afraid that you were going to give me crap for being a baby," Charles said smiling.

A nurse walked in carrying a metal cane. Laurie took the cane, thanked her, and the nurse left as quickly as she'd come. Laurie tossed a pair of brown Quicksilver flip-flops at Charles' feet. "Here, slip these on."

Charles put on the sandals and took the cane. He took a couple of steps. "I feel ridiculous."

Laurie grinned mischievously. "You look ridiculous but it has nothing to do with the cane."

11

Laurie parked her police cruiser behind the Edgartown Library and stepped out onto the gravel lot. She closed her door behind her and walked around to the passenger side. Charles opened his door, pushing hard enough for the weight to swing it open on its own. Laurie reached in and Charles took her hand, mostly for leverage. He swung his legs out and dug his cane into the gravel. With some effort, he stood up.

"I hope this gets easier really quickly!" Charles shook his head in frustration.

"It will get easier as you get healthier. Don't stress over it," Laurie said supportively. "That won't help you." She closed the car door behind him.

"I'll do my best." Charles walked with the handle of the cane planted firmly in his left palm. Once he got going, it wasn't that bad. Getting in and out of cars was tough. He was also a little concerned about the stairs leading up to the Edgartown Inn porch; however, there was no point in trying to avoid them. At some point, stairs would be inevitable no matter where they went.

They walked slowly down the red brick path in front of the Edgartown Library to the sidewalk on North Water Street. The Edgartown Inn was right next-door. Charles wished they were turning in the other direction and heading toward Fuller Street Beach but he feared that his swimming days were over for at least a little while.

Having reached the base of the stairs, Charles grabbed the railing. "Here goes nothing." He planted the cane on the first step and pushed down. He took the step with a little more ease than he was expecting. "That was pretty good, actually."

"What, in God's name, have you done to yourself?" Edie stepped out onto the porch of her inn with a horrified look on her face.

Charles pointed at Laurie. "She hit me!" he exclaimed. Charles took another two steps up.

"I did not!" Laurie exclaimed, rolling her eyes at Edie. "However the temptation is getting stronger all the time."

Charles stood on the porch and straightened his back. "Good morning, Edie."

"Good morning. Now, what the hell happened to you?" Edie pulled open the screen door and stepped back to let Charles go first. "Go through and get a table. I'll bring you both some coffee and cake and then you are going to tell me exactly what's going on."

"We're here to talk about the wedding, Edie." Charles said walking through the front vestibule.

"That's fine but if you think I'm going to sit around talking tea lights and prime rib while you're sitting across the table from me looking like you just limped in off the set of Apocalypse Now, you've got another think coming!" Once Edie had decided something there was very little that could be done to change her mind.

"That's fair enough." Laurie agreed.

"Thank you." Edie's tone relaxed. She watched Charles move gingerly through the dining room. "Oh, you poor thing. Be careful, the ground is uneven out there." Charles walked through the back door into the back garden. Edie clasped her face between her hands. "I can hardly watch. I'm going to get you your coffees."

Charles made out reasonably well on the uneven ground of the Edgartown Inn patio. He pulled out his usual chair under the big maple tree in the corner and sat down. Laurie sat across from him. They hadn't been in their seats for a minute when Edie came with their coffees and cake. She turned to a neighbouring table to ask if she may take the empty chair. Charles watched

122

as Edie's smile burst onto her face and her eyes ignited with animation. When the guests agreed, Edie laughed her gratitude, turned the chair toward Charles and Laurie, and turned her head to face them, her smile extinguished and the animation behind her eyes dulled. Years of hotel work had designed and installed a marquee on top of Edie's personality; it turned on and off—it was there for the patrons.

"Okay," Edie said in a no-nonsense tone. She looked at Charles and then at Laurie. "What's going on?"

Charles and Laurie took turns telling Edie the story of the morning's events. Charles tried to give a detailed report of what had happened up until he passed out in Farm Pond and Laurie took over when the two joggers had found Charles' phone and subsequently, found Charles. Charles listened as intently as Edie did when Laurie spoke. He hadn't heard this part of the story yet and had questions of his own. According to Laurie, the two joggers called 911 and emergency services dispatched an ambulance and a police car to the scene. The two joggers were standing by the pond keeping an eye on him when they arrived. Sergeant Jack Burrell was the officer on scene and he waded into the pond with one of the emergency medical men from the ambulance and pulled him out. Once Charles was out of the water and loaded into the ambulance, Jack called Laurie and told her to meet them at Martha's Vineyard Hospital. Jack then went back into the pond for Charles' shoes.

"When Jack showed up at the hospital, he looked like he'd spent the afternoon mud wrestling," Laurie chuckled.

"Talk about going above and beyond," Edie said. "He's a good kid. That was such a tragedy, what happened to him last summer—losing a young wife like that. It breaks my heart."

"Mine too." Laurie agreed. "At least if we had found a body he could have had closure but we never did. He seems to be doing pretty good though—he still has his moments. Jack's a really good police officer though, I'll give him that."

The events of the previous summer flashed through Charles' mind. Charles, Jeff, and Laurie had uncovered the Zito brothers' smuggling illegal shark fins through the Monster Shark Fishing Tournament. Chief Jeffries had been shot and in the act of saving him, their friend Gavin had lost a leg to a great white shark. Jack Burrell had lost his wife—Marcie—to the same shark. The murders at JAWSfest had been a year before that. A sane man would never return to Martha's Vineyard but as much as Charles had found it all terrifying, it had been exhilarating at the same time. The rest of his life seemed dull and lacklustre by comparison. There was also Laurie to consider. Charles looked at her and smiled.

124

"I don't understand what anyone would possibly have to gain from killing you, Charles. What a horrible thing. I can't even bear to think about it," Edie said with an expression that betrayed both puzzlement and horror.

"I'm not thrilled about it either, Edie," Charles said. "What makes it so difficult is that we have no idea what they wanted, so we have no idea how to proceed. All we can do is try and track down the SUV."

"We'll drive up to Oak Bluffs later to see how they're making out on their end," Laurie said. "They'll need some time first."

"So, Edie, what's going on with the wedding?" Charles asked. "Let's have some good news for a change."

Edie shot Laurie a knowing look and then turned to Charles. "I think it's going well! The tables will be covered with white tablecloths and there will be a cluster of tea lights on each table in a circle of yellow roses from Donaroma's. The yellow roses will be the same as the roses in Laurie's bouquet. We chose yellow because yellow symbolizes friendship. I thought that was a nice tribute to how you two got together."

"I think it's cool too." Charles nodded.

"Oh good. I'm glad," Edie said. "We also have patio lanterns that are really pretty. They're made out of wine bottles! The bottom is removed and the strand of lights is inserted through the neck. They have a real country feel."

"They're not too tacky? They sound kind of tacky." Charles wasn't convinced.

"I don't think so." Edie took the criticism in stride. "You said that you wanted a more casual feel."

"Yes, casual for a wedding not a barn dance!"

"Charles!" Laurie said.

"No. Edie, I didn't mean to be rude. I just think that the lights sound a little *too* casual for a wedding."

Edie talked with her hands. "Nope! No problem at all. It's important that you be honest with me or you guys won't get the wedding you want and then you'll resent me for it and I'll feel terrible." She smiled and squeezed Charles' hand affectionately. "If you didn't say what was on your mind, I'd never forgive you. Okay, about the food."

"Yes, food!" Laurie took a bite of her coffee cake.

"Prime rib dinner done buffet style work for you guys? It's a small group. Everyone should be able to get all they need very quickly, don't you think?" Edie scanned both of their faces for recognition.

Laurie and Charles nodded. "Agreed."

"Good. That's easy. I have asked Alexandra and Mary to serve and clear. They're always asking for extra hours so it works out nicely." Edie made a note in her book. Her loose curls fell over her face as she wrote.

"Oh by the way, Edie, we invited Dr and Barbara Nevin this morning. Can you give them a call? If we're getting married in the garden at The Edgartown Inn, the Nevins should be there. Don't you think?" Laurie suggested.

"I think that's a lovely idea," Edie said. "Charles you're going to have to give up your favourite seat. This is the Nevins' table!"

"As long as it's only for one day," Charles smiled. He took another bite of cake and washed it down with some coffee. The sun shone into the garden and danced on the guests as they ate their breakfast. The branches swayed with a musical rhythm. In the back of his mind, Charles heard Ravel's Bolero. Laurie and Edie continued to talk about wedding plans but Charles drifted away. It was easy for him to get lost in the flowers that Edie had so meticulously planted around the garden, in the greenery and in the red brick, in the yellow of the sun. Yet somewhere on Martha's Vineyard, someone wanted Charles dead.

*   *   *

The Edgartown Police Station was bustling when Laurie and Charles walked in. Outside, Charles had opted to use the ramp instead of the stairs, more out of curiosity than anything else. In the end, he decided that the stairs weren't that hard and that the ramp took too long. Charles knew that Laurie barely tolerated these curious experiments of his; however, she understood his need to compare things intellectually. Charles had a need to experience even the most trivial of things for himself and store those experiences away to be used as a frame of reference in the future. Information was never a waste. So, Laurie took the stairs and then waited for Charles at the front door of the station while he walked up the ramp with his cane, absorbing every minute. When Charles finally reached the door, Laurie was standing with her computer bag over her shoulder, the door propped open with her foot, and an eyebrow arched in mild indignation.

"Hi, Chief! Hi, Charles!" Sergeant Jack Burrell smiled at them with genuine exuberance as they walked in. His thick dark eyebrows lifted and his eyes squinted over a broad toothy smile. It was a smile that Charles couldn't help but return. He doubted anyone could.

"Jack! It's good to see you." Charles limped into the main foyer of the station and Jack came around the desk.

"How are you making out? Jeez! That guy really did a number on you, didn't he? God. I got your shoes; I gave them to Chief Knickles. I think she's washing them. Well, she would have to be washing them—they were a real mess. I did a race once in Boston called Tough Mudder and your shoes looked worse than mine when I was done!" Jack laughed while he talked. Charles doubted that he was even aware of it.

"I hear you were a real mess after you dug them out!" Charles reached out and shook Jack's hand. "Thanks for that, Jack. That really means a lot; I love my Nike SHOX. You'll have to let me buy you a beer at The Newes of America."

"I'd love it! That would be great! You don't have to buy though. I was happy to do it. I would want someone to get my shoes for me! I have those Vibrams. You know, the ones with the individual toe slots? They're supposed to be so good for your feet. I don't know if they really are or not. It's probably just a gimmick. I haven't noticed—"

"*It is a guy thing,*" Laurie said quietly shaking her head. When she spoke again, her tone was more commanding and professional. "Sergeant," she said.

The sergeant looked sheepish. "Sorry."

Charles laughed and patted the sergeant on the shoulder. "It's so good to see you, Jack," Charles said. "You haven't changed a bit."

"Truer words have never been spoken," Laurie said. "Sergeant, we'll be in my office."

"Okay Chief," Jack said. "Good to see you too, Charles. I really want to go for that beer!"

"Me too! Definitely!" Charles followed Laurie down the hall to her office. They walked at almost a regular pace. Charles' joints were sore, particularly his knees, but he was pleased that he was able to keep up to her with relative ease. Laurie sat in the black leather chair behind her desk and Charles made himself comfortable in one of the chairs facing her. He propped his left leg up on the vacant chair beside him. Straightening the knee and elevating his foot felt wonderful.

Laurie pulled her computer out of her bag and set it on her desk. The screen sprung to life when she opened it. She typed what Charles imagined to be a password and then reached into her breast pocket for her glasses. Once her glasses were perched on her nose, she slid them down as far as they could go and even then pulled her head back from the screen. She turned and looked up at Charles. He was staring at her quizzically.

"I really need a new prescription," she said.

"Apparently." Charles grinned.

Laurie picked up a pile of pink and white papers from the desk on her left and began to read them. When she had finished, she pushed down the intercom button on her desk phone. "Jack can you come in here please and get me up to speed?"

"You know, I don't have to sit here all day," Charles said.

"Someone tried to kill you this morning and I'm not really sure what to do with you right now," Laurie said. Neither her voice nor her face showed a trace of humour. "Doesn't that concern you?"

130

"Well, yes but I was walking alone on a deserted street very early in the morning. The island is much busier now that it is mid-day. I think if I stick to crowded areas and ride buses, I'll be fine. Don't you?"

"Probably," Laurie said. Doing her best to suppress her anxiety and worry made Laurie's voice deeper than usual. She spoke without looking up. Her hands flipped through the papers but she wasn't reading them. "Charles, I'm sorry if it seems like I'm over-reacting but I already lost one husband, remember?" Her face had become quite sombre. I'd really prefer not to lose another one."

Charles felt his limbs go numb. It hadn't even dawned on him. How could he be so inconsiderate? On the first day that they had reconnected on Martha's Vineyard, Laurie had told him that a drunk driver had killed her first husband, Mark. That conversation had been two years ago now and they hadn't talked about it since. Charles had forgotten all about it. Of course, Laurie would be drawing parallels. How could she not? As soon as Jack had called her, while she had been racing to get to his side at the hospital, she would have been thinking about Mark. The entire experience, all of her feelings that she had buried years ago would have been exhumed in an instant—graveolant, feculent, and noxious memories all resurrected and laid just behind her eyes demanding that she pay her respects. Yet, she hadn't said anything to him. Her focus had been strictly on Charles.

"Laurie, I'm so sorry." Charles' emotions rolled from embarrassment to sympathy. "I didn't even think. Of course you'd be thinking of Mark."

Laurie continued to shuffle her office memos. "Why would you? It didn't happen to you. It didn't happen to your husband. This morning, *that* happened to you. That's what you should have on your mind. It's what I'm thinking about too, Charles. I just wanted to explain why I might be a little more sensitive on the subject. Maybe I shouldn't have brought it up but a really big part of me doesn't want to let you out of my sight *ever*. Wouldn't you feel the same way?"

Charles smiled. "I don't want to let you out of my sight now."

Laurie looked up from her papers. She smiled with sincere appreciation. Her eyes were glassy.

"Yes," said Charles. "I would feel the same way."

"Thank you."

Jack walked in the open door of Laurie's office. "Hi, Chief." Jack's face had always struck Charles as a shiny new penny when he had first met him. Now, since the events of last summer and the death of Jack's wife, Marcie, his face still shone but it was a bit tarnished. It hadn't lost any of its value but the freshness had faded—last year's currency.

"What's been going on, Jack?" The springs in Laurie's chair protested as she reclined.

"Not a whole lot, Chief." Jack began to read from a yellow note pad. "There was a domestic violence call out Katama way; some off-islanders had too much to drink. She spent the night in the drunk-tank. Ben Masters has been complaining about kids out his way. Trespassing on his fields. He says they spook his cows. We sent a patrol out there. Someone had been out there but we didn't catch anyone. I told him that we would keep an eye out. I asked him to let us know if he sees anything else."

"I doubt you had to tell him that," said Laurie. "He's never had a problem speaking up!"

"That's true enough." Jack nodded his head in agreement and flipped to the next page of his note pad. "Other than that, it's been really quiet. Mrs Hakala called us four times because she couldn't find her glasses. I know that I should be telling her not to call us for things like that but I just walk over to her house on my lunch and find them for her. They're usually out in the open somewhere. Once they were on her head! I don't mind doing it; she's such a nice old lady."

"You don't mind doing it because she gives you homemade baking every time you go!" Laurie winked at him. "Admit it!"

Jack blushed and chuckled boyishly. "Sometimes twice a day!"

"Oh well, what are old ladies for if not to fatten up young bachelors?" Laurie said offhandedly. An awkward silence fell over the office. "I'm sorry, Jack. That was insensitive of me." She looked up at her sergeant.

Jack smiled. "That's okay, Chief. Marcie's been gone a year now. Besides, she was a nice girl but she never was much of a baker." Jack tried feebly to inject humour into the situation but his words fell limp with emotion at the mention of his dead wife. His already youthful face took on a child-like quality that reminded Charles of watching a baby sleeping. There was innocence there. He smiled softly. "I'd probably still be trying to score baking out of Mrs Hakala."

"I know I would be! I am totally jealous! You have any of this baking here with you?" Charles winked at Jack and lifting the pall that had briefly fallen over the office.

"I didn't even think of that!" Laurie exclaimed. "Do you?"

"No, I don't. Sorry," Jack said. "Next time! I usually share with the guys anyway."

"You share Mrs Hakala's baking with the guys and this is the first I've heard of it?" Laurie exclaimed.

Jack chuckled nervously.

"Jack, I sign your paycheques. You might want to rethink your cookie distribution. That's all I'm sayin'." Laurie stared at him, deadpan.

Jack shifted his balance from one foot to the other, not really sure what to say or do next.

"Jack," Laurie said. "I'm kidding."

Jack grinned sheepishly. "I knew that," he lied.

"Sure you did," Laurie said. "Jack I don't even sign your paycheques."

"Right! I guess you don't," he said.

"...But I can fire you," Laurie said straight-faced.

Charles looked at Laurie with a sardonic grin. "You're a horrible little person."

12

Laurie picked up her phone on the first ring. She spoke briefly and then hung up. Laurie had been taking care of paperwork while Charles surfed the Internet on his iPhone, listening on small earphones that fit neatly in his ears. They had spent the last couple of hours quietly sitting at her desk. Neither of them had spoken a word. Charles found the quiet very comforting. He hadn't realised how much he needed some down time. There was something intoxicating about the comfort level required to sit in silence with another human being for a long period of time—longer than four minutes anyway, thought Charles. Laurie looked up and waved to get his attention. It worked and he pulled out an earphone.

"Want to go up to Oak Bluffs?" Laurie asked him.

"Sure. Why?"

"Well, I think I'm going to be here a while. I don't want to be but I really should be. I'll feel better when I get all of this cleared up." Laurie motioned to the piles of paper still on her desk. There were more piles than there had been the last time Charles had looked up but the piles were smaller and seemed more organised. "Jeff is in town and offered to pick you up. You know what they say, 'a change is as good as a break'," she said.

"So, I'm just being shifted from one police station to another?" Charles furrowed his brow.

"No, Jeff can take you home if you like." Laurie looked like she had given the matter a lot of thought. "It's not fair to keep you under constant surveillance."

Charles smiled. "I'll be fine."

"I know," Laurie said. "Text me a few million times though would ya?"

"No problem." Charles unplugged his earphones, wrapped them around his hand, and put them in his pocket.

"What were you watching?" Laurie asked.

"An FBI lecture on poisons at San Francisco University."

Laurie shook her head. "Of course you were."

"Is Jeff on his way now?" asked Charles.

Laurie nodded. "He'll probably be outside by the time you get out there."

Charles stood up and grabbed his cane. He leaned in to kiss Laurie good-bye. "See you later."

She kissed him. "I'll text you when I'm done."

When Charles pushed open the front door of the police station, Jeff was sitting out front in his cruiser just as Laurie had predicted.

This time, Charles opted for the stairs as he left rather than the long ramp that he had used to enter the station. He was mastering the cane quite well. As he approached the car, Jeff leaned over and opened the passenger door. Charles slipped into the passenger seat and pulled the door shut. He looked at his friend. "Chief Jefferies," he said.

"Mr Williams," said Jeff.

"Where to?"

"Well, that's up to you," said Jeff. "I can either take you home or..."

"Yes?"

"...Or I can take you to Mrs Beacham's with me."

"You're going to Violet Beacham's now?" Charles asked.

"I have a four o'clock appointment, remember?" Jeff said. "I don't want to be late."

"Well, if my options are sitting in Violet Beacham's driveway or hanging at home with my friends, I think I'll choose the latter." Charles smiled a somewhat dejected smile.

"Actually, I thought you might want to come in with me."

Charles' eyes lit up. "In what capacity?"

"You were the only one who was at Sam's first accident and you were on the scene for his last accident. You might have some valuable input. I remember Laurie deputizing you last summer; I don't think that we'll need to go to that extreme but you're observant and smart. Questions might come up regarding the night that Sam rolled his car outside your house; gaps that will be easier to fill if I have you and Mrs Beacham together in the same room."

"How will Violet Beacham feel about that?" asked Charles.

Jeff shrugged. "There's only one way to find out," he said. "She's ornery, that's for sure but if you follow a certain protocol, she's not that bad. Laurie doesn't get it because she's from America—sorry, the mainland," Jeff said. "I was born here; it's an islander thing." Jeff put the cruiser in drive and the car rolled down the driveway to Peases Point Way. "So, where are we going?"

"Well, I know that Laurie would feel a lot better if I was under police surveillance." Charles grinned.

"Mrs Beacham's it is."

They drove up Peases Point until Jeff turned right onto Upper Main Street. This street is always busy, thought Charles. There were probably some times in the small hours of the morning that it was quiet but if the summer sun was high enough—it was busy. Charles wondered how much of the traffic was local and how much of it was tourist. The season had started and statistics showed that Martha's Vineyard's population grew from fifteen thousand to one hundred and twenty thousand in the summer. That meant, in theory, that one in every eight cars was local. Charles found wrapping his head around that fact to be difficult. In the distance, Charles saw a flicker of red metal glimmer in the sun and his whole body tightened. It was coming toward them in the oncoming traffic. There were eight or ten cars in front of it, cars of grey, beige, and blue but then without mistake, sitting a little taller than all of the cars was a red truck. Charles felt his chest tighten. Every muscle in his body flexed. He felt his face flush.

"Charles?" Jeff asked.

Charles realised then that Jeff had been speaking to him but Charles hadn't heard him. He had been focussed on the truck and nothing else. Charles' eyes burned from not blinking.

"*Charles?*" Jeff asked again with a more urgent tone. "*Charles, what's the matter with you?*"

Charles forced himself to inhale and exhale deeply. The oxygen lubricated his muscles and the tension broke away from his chest like rust on twisting metal. Still, Charles would not take his eyes off the red truck.

"There's a red SUV coming toward us," Charles said. He pointed through the windshield.

Jeff followed Charles' gaze and his finger. He saw the truck. "Is it your truck, Charles? Do you want me to stop him?"

They both watched it go by. Charles looked at the front grill; it was in mint condition. The whole truck in fact, upon closer inspection, was wrong. It was too new. Even Charles could see that. The edges were too round and the truck itself was too compact. The truck that had come after him was squarer. It was bigger and meaner looking if that made any sense.

"*Charles? Is it your truck?*" Jeff demanded.

Charles shook his head. "No. No, it's not."

Jeff let out an exasperated sigh. "Alright then. Say something next time would ya? You're freakin' me out!"

"Sorry." Charles twisted in his seat to watch the truck pass by.

"Are you alright?" Jeff asked.

Charles nodded. "Yes. I'm fine." Charles sat back in his seat properly. "Do me a favour would you? Don't tell Laurie about this."

Jeff chuckled and shook his head. "I'm not making any promises, buddy." The two men sat quietly for a moment, mulling over what had just happened. "I tell you what, if Laurie asks me any questions—I won't lie to her but I won't volunteer the information either."

Charles nodded. "That's fair."

"I *am* going to take you home though." Jeff said. "I think you could use the rest. You either need a nap or just to chill with a couple of friends, have a beer, a few laughs, something to take your mind off of all of this."

Charles was disappointed but he didn't argue. "There's probably something in that. Take me home but fill me in later. I would like to hear what Violet has to say."

"I will. I'm sure that I'll have some questions for you when I'm done and I know that Laurie will be curious to hear about it too."

Charles leaned forward and turned on the radio. His hope was that it would take some of the pressure off having to make conversation. The four-minute silence wouldn't be long enough for him right now. MVY Radio was playing *Band On The Run* by *Wings*. Charles had always loved that song and he tried to sing along but he didn't have it in him. It was a happy-sounding song but inside, Charles was stewing. His heart was still racing from seeing the red truck. The fact that he had reacted so strongly upset him more than the actual truck had. It seemed that the incident on Beach Road had shaken him up more than he was willing to admit but why shouldn't it? It was a big admission to say that someone actually wanted you dead.

*   *   *

Jeff drove the police cruiser into the driveway on Pondview Drive and put it in neutral behind Brad's green Subaru Outback. Brad's license plates read JAWS*75. That always made Charles smile. The house was quiet out front and Charles assumed that all of the action—if there was any action—was going on out back on the deck. He opened the car door and was hit by the intoxicating smell of meat grilling on a barbecue. A burger and a beer would go down nicely, he thought.

"Well, here you go—home sweet home." Jeff leaned forward to get a better look at the house through the windshield. "Give me a shout if you need anything," he said. "I know that Laurie probably told you the same thing but if it's anything serious, I'm closer."

"Alright. Thanks." Charles stood his crutch up on the driveway and pulled himself up with it. His knees and hips hurt as they straightened. They were stiff from the car ride. Charles felt like his was in the advanced stages of arthritis. "Actually, I'm glad that I'm here. It will be good to spend some more time with these guys."

"That's what I figured. Probably do you the world of good," Jeff said. "Anyway, call me if you need anything."

"I will," said Charles. He stepped back and gave the door a push. It closed with a mechanical click. The car pulled away and Jeff drove back toward Barnes Road. When the hum of the car engine had faded, Charles was left standing in the natural quiet. His body was still but his eyes roamed. The Atlantic wind whispered through the leaves on its journey across the island before dropping off the Aquinnah cliffs and back to the sea. Green leaves danced with yellow sunlight, syncopating their black and brown branches. Charles stood hypnotised by the chiaroscuro.

The calm was broken by a happy guffaw emanating from the other side of the house. Charles recognised it as Brooke. He grinned at the thought of his friend and turned in the direction of her laughter. Rather than cutting through the house, he opted to go around. There was no well-travelled path so the ground was soft under his feet. An outdoor shower was fixed to the house but spider webs, leaves, and twigs betrayed its lack of use. Past the shower were the cellar door and a rather large pile of firewood. Charles found it fascinating that every summer rental on the Internet boasted an outdoor shower. He wondered if any of the others were used more than this one.

As he rounded the side of the house, Charles saw his friends on the back deck. Brad, Brooke, and Kevin were sitting in green Adirondack chairs much as they had been the last time he had seen them. This time,

Charles' friends, Tina Simms and Matthew Lake, were there as well. Charles' grin widened. This was a total surprise! He had no idea that they were going to be on the Vineyard. Matthew used to live on the island but had moved to Cape Cod last summer. Tina lived in Massachusetts but in Springfield. It wasn't like either of them had come from England like Brooke had, but still Charles hadn't been expecting them. Matthew saw Charles first.

"There he is!" Matthew stood and raised a Sam Adams in his direction. "Hey dude! It's about time you got here!"

Charles hurried his pace as much as he could.

"Christ, man, what did you do to your leg?" Matthew watched Charles as he pushed himself up the deck steps with his cane.

"Don't look at me—I didn't do it," Charles said.

Brooke rushed over to him and took his hand. "Bloody hell, sit down, luv! What happened?"

Charles let Brooke lead him to a chair and he sat down. Something about being pampered made him play it up—it was reflex.

"Do you want me to make you a cup of tea or are you up for something stronger?"

Charles laughed. "Only you would offer me a cup of tea. I think I'll have something stronger."

"What would you like, luv?" Brooke rubbed his shoulder in a motherly fashion.

"Would you make me a Rusty Nail?" Charles asked.

This time, Brooke laughed. "And you tease me for being British! You're not far off! I'm going to make you an honorary Brit! Of course I will make you a Rusty Nail, luv. You just rest up and I'll be right back."

"What the Christ is a Rusty Nail?" Matthew asked.

"Two to one, Scotch and Drambuie," said Charles.

"What's Drambuie?" Kevin asked.

"It's a liqueur distilled from Scotch," said Charles.

"That sounds disgusting!" Tina said.

"It's actually very sweet. I'll let you try mine."

"I'll drink one!" Matthew said.

"You'll drink turpentine if I let you!" Tina laughed.

"What's your point?" Matt chuckled.

"What are you guys even doing here? I had no idea that you were coming!" Charles looked at Tina and Matthew. They sat facing Charles on the other side of the cheap metal and glass patio table.

"We didn't exactly know that we were coming either. It was a last minute thing. Matthew called me because his plans fell through and by sheer coincidence, mine fell through just before he called. So, here we are!"

"Yeah, I was supposed to go out tagging great whites with Ocearch but the trip got postponed." Matthew shrugged.

Tina was small, blonde, and spritely. Charles hadn't seen her since JAWSfest two years ago. That was the last time he had seen Matthew as well; however, they had kept in daily contact via Facebook. Social media had really changed personal relationships. Charles felt closer to some of these people than most of the people he saw in person on a daily basis.

"*Well... what happened to you?*" Kevin asked.

Charles told them the story of the red truck and his visit to the hospital. They all sat in silence, thoroughly engrossed.

Brooke set his drink down in front of him when he was finished. She had been mixing his drink just inside the screen door listening intently and had been too engrossed or upset by his words to think to set it down before he finished. When she leaned forward over him, a tear fell from her eye and landed on the table. She swiped at her cheek instinctively. "That's just terrible," Brooke said. "Why would someone do that to you? Why would someone want to hurt you like that? You're such a dear man. You've not done anything to anyone. You're on bloody holiday to get married!"

"I agree. I don't get it," said Brad. His tone was one of equal concern but less emotional than Brooke's. "If you were in Toronto, it might make more sense. Not that someone would have a legitimate reason to harm you but at least you would have an established network there. Here, on this island, who do you even know?"

"It's a fair point," Charles said. "But it's a question that I cannot answer, at least not yet. Your guess is as good as mine."

"There's always the possibility that he wasn't trying to kill you, just scare you," Kevin said. "I mean you are still here."

Charles looked at his friend thoughtfully and sipped his Rusty Nail. The drink was cold, sweet, and almost thick. The Drambuie thickened it, slowing its movement. When he looked through the glass, he could actually see it lethargically wrapping itself around the ice cubes. Charles always felt that he had to pull the first sip of a Rusty Nail through his mouth to help it find its way; otherwise, the alcoholic sweetness would just pool there lazily. "That's true," he said finally. "If someone really wanted me dead, there are certainly more efficient ways to do it than trying to mow me down with a truck. There's plenty of cover along that road, someone could have taken me out with one shot. But scare me from what?"

"I haven't got a clue, buddy," Kevin said.

"One more thing—remember Sam Grover?" Charles asked.

"How can I forget?" Brad said.

"I'll never forget it either!" said Brooke. She shuddered. "That bloke gave me the fright of my life, he did."

"Well, he won't scare you anymore," Charles said. "He's dead. He drove his car off the Gay Head Cliffs last night."

There was silence. No one had a response. Charles always thought that it was comical when people were shocked into silence, comical but not funny. Everyone stared back at him with blank saucer faces. Charles was reminded of that ridiculous act on Ed Sullivan where an "artist" spun several plates on sticks. That's what he saw. Spinning white plates on sticks, ridiculous, blank, and not funny. Charles' plate was spinning right along with them. He had no answers either.

"*Jesus!*" Brad said.

"I know. Chief Jefferies of Oak Bluffs called Laurie and me out there when we were headed out for dinner last night. We don't know how or why it happened," said Charles.

"That poor boy." Brooke shook her head with a mother's sympathy.

"Sam Grover's accident here and then his death last night are the only things that have happened that were out of the ordinary. Now someone has tried to kill me—or at least scare me as Adam pointed out. If the events are part and parcel, I can't see what's tying them together."

"Maybe it's just a coincidence?" Tina suggested.

Charles shook his head. "I've never believed in coincidence."

"Well, you're here now," Kevin said. "Nothing's going to happen when we're all here together."

"I agree with Adam," said Tina. "Let's try and focus on the positive. We never get together and now that we're here we should try and enjoy ourselves. I'm sure that Laurie and Chief Jefferies are working overtime to figure this out. Let's at least try to have a good time together."

"That's why Jeff dropped me here actually. He said I should let off some steam. Enjoy some quality friend time!" Charles grinned.

"Then that's what we'll do!" Tina smiled. "Tell us about the wedding!"

"It should be pretty cool, actually!" Charles smiled at the thought of it. "It's taking place entirely at the Edgartown Inn. Our friend Edie is organising it."

"Is she your wedding planner?" Tina asked.

"Well, kind of. She's the manager of the Edgartown Inn and a friend; it seemed a natural fit. She knows the inn better than anyone. So when it comes to questions of seating capacity, kitchen capabilities, so on and so forth, she will be able to sort things out. It's such a great space."

150

"What about the other guests?" Brad asked.

"There won't be any. We booked it for the weekend," said Charles. "So, it will be empty. We didn't want to bother anyone and we won't inconvenience Edie's business either."

"*You booked the whole inn?*" Brooke exclaimed. "Bloody hell! That must have cost you a few quid!"

Charles shrugged. "We got a deal."

"What are we having to eat?" Kevin asked.

"Prime rib buffet," said Charles. "We just decided that yesterday actually."

"Sounds delish!" Tina said.

"Tell me there's gonna be an open bar! There's gonna be an open bar right, Charles?" Matthew laughed as he spoke but everyone knew he really wanted one.

"*Open bar for you?? Who am I—Donald Trump??*" Charles scoffed. Everyone laughed.

"Come on!!" Matthew exclaimed.

"We're working on it," Charles placated. "We'll figure out something."

"Oh, it's going to be brilliant!" Brooke said.

"I hope so," Charles said. "The people will all be great. It's a really small crowd. I think that's the most important part of any gathering."

"What about music?" Brad asked.

"I'm not sure," Charles said. "I'll have to ask Edie. I'm sure she's got it covered. Still, it hasn't come up when I've been there. If I know Laurie, she's put in a request for a lot of eighties music!" Charles pulled out his iPhone and made himself a note. "I'll bring it up tomorrow."

Charles sat back in his chair and enjoyed the scene playing out before him. Matthew told them all about the latest painting he was working on—a great white shark breaching the waters off the Massachusetts coast—and Kevin tried to talk them all into getting up before the crack of dawn to go fishing the next morning. No one was willing to commit to a 5:00 a.m. call. Brooke hovered and buzzed like a hummingbird refreshing drinks; Charles' glass was refilled more than a few times. She flipped burgers, and turned over sausages. It was quite the scene and everyone played his or her part. Jeff had been right; it was exactly what Charles needed. Charles believed that the more intense the stress, the bigger the party required. There had to be balance in the galaxy.

13

The cab driver had no problem pulling into the driveway as it was well lit by the porch light. Most of the taxis on Martha's Vineyard were large white vans and this one was no exception. It made sense when Charles thought about it. All of the cabs had to be ready to carry couples and/or families with a lot of luggage. Charles imagined that being a four-door sedan taxi on a vacation destination would cut back on fares dramatically. When the taxi came to a full stop, the driver pressed firmly on the horn twice.

Charles and his friends poured out of the front door of the house laughing and yelling. They were living proof that there was a direct correlation between alcohol consumed and volume of speech.

Charles stayed on the veranda while his friends stepped onto the lawn and staggered toward the van.

"Are you sure you won't come with us?" Kevin asked. "You don't have to play pool; you can just hang out, have a pint."

"No—thanks. I think I need to go to bed. It's been a long day. You guys have fun," Charles said.

Kevin laughed watching the rest of the gang totter toward the van. "I don't think that will be a problem!" He turned to catch up with the others. "See you tomorrow!"

Charles nodded in agreement. The driver got out of the front seat and ran barefoot around the van. The sight of him made Charles laugh. In Toronto, the cabbies were all corpulent middle-eastern men who smelled of sweat and cigar smoke. The fit white college kids driving their vans barefoot in nothing but a t-shirt and shorts did not fit the image of a cabbie by any stretch of Charles' imagination. The cabbie pulled open the side door and helped the motley crew pile in. When they were all more or less settled on a seat, he slid the door closed, ran back around the van, and hopped up into his seat. As the cab pulled out of the driveway, Charles raised a hand and waved them off. They disappeared into the night but Charles could hear their drunken screams and cackles for a few seconds longer than he could see them.

Charles stood and leaned against a wood post that held up the porch roof. He'd had more than a couple of Rusty Nails throughout the evening and his

154

fair share of Sam Adams as well. That was enough alcohol to lubricate his sore hips and knees and still have enough leftover to make him forget about his scrapes and bruises too. He felt good. Charles stood in the quiet and took in the trees and the night. There was no car crash, there were no flashing lights, and there were no young men running out of the darkness. This night was what a Martha's Vineyard night should be—quiet and calm. Charles inhaled deeply. His lungs expanded to their limit sucking in all of the sweet country air that they could, and then almost immediately, expelling it as quickly as it had come. Satisfied with the silence and the dark, Charles turned and went inside.

The house was bright. They had left all of the lights on. There wasn't a shadow in any corner. The table had been cleared for the most part; the dishes were in the sink but there were wine glasses and beer cans still on the table. The coffee table still had dishes on it. They belonged to Jamie. Jamie naturally was on the couch. He had been sitting up and been part of the conversation toward the end of the night but now with the party gone, he was stretched out and staring back at the television.

"Are you finished with those?" Charles asked.

"What?" Jamie's eyes remained on the TV.

"Your dishes, Jamie, are you finished with them?" Charles asked.

"Oh yeah, you can take them dude—thanks," Jamie said.

Charles thought briefly that he should tell Jamie to clear his own goddamn dishes but at the last moment he thought better of it. He and Jamie were alone in the house for the night. Charles didn't want to spend what should be his quiet evening at home arguing with him. He bent over and took the plate, cutlery, and beer bottle. Jamie didn't move.

The kitchen could be in much worse shape, Charles thought. He opened the dishwasher and began to fill it methodically. Plates first, then pots, glassware, mugs, and finally cutlery. When it came to the cutlery he put in all of the spoons, then all of the forks, then knives, finishing with larger knives and serving spoons. Charles had come up with this procedure when he was much younger and he had always stuck with it— bottom tray first larger dishes before smaller then upper tray with glassware and mugs. Cutlery started with spoons, they were short and round. If he put the forks or knives in first, he was constantly jabbing himself. The longer utensils like serving spoons and carving knives went in last to avoid hindering him from putting in the shorter items. Once full, Charles dropped in a square of soap and closed the dishwasher door. He turned it on and left it to run. The kitchen counter got his attention next and then the dining room table. Outside, through his reflection in the sliding glass door,

Charles could see an overflowing ashtray on the deck table. He slid the door open and stepped outside.

The air was cool and fresh but soured with the smell of the ashtray. Charles grimaced. Like almost all non-smokers, Charles was repulsed by the smell of cigarettes and ashtrays were even worse. He stepped back inside and inspected the ashtray closely. Once he was satisfied that there were no burning embers, that the contents were cold, he dumped it into the green garbage bag just inside the door. He walked to the kitchen sink, gave it a good wipe, and brought it back outside to the cheap glass table on the deck. Charles felt the night walk through him. He felt naked and exposed. The hair stood up on Charles' neck. He turned around. There was nothing but trees. Branches reached toward him randomly out of the dark. Through the trees' silhouette he could see the glow of the neighbours front light. It was the house where he and Laurie had returned Adam Haliburton's mail to his sister Mandy. The house was a good distance away and their light didn't illuminate much. Charles rotated a slow one hundred and eighty degrees. His chest tightened. He felt like the fish that instinctively darted away moments before the shark swam onto the scene. He could see nothing. Goose flesh rose on his arm but still there was no sign of anything alarming. He folded his arms across his chest in a protective barrier against the cold and his imagination. Was it his imagination?

Or was it instinct? Either way, Charles couldn't shake the feeling that someone was watching him, that there was someone standing in the darkness, waiting, and watching.

Charles stepped back inside and closed the sliding glass door. He locked it and felt foolish for doing so. Even if there were someone out in the woods watching him, the lock on a sliding glass door would offer him very little protection. He remembered being a teenager and breaking into the sliding glass door on his parents' house many times when he had forgotten his key. Charles locked the door anyway. There was no curtain on the door. Why would there be? The backyard was completely private. Under normal circumstances, curtains or blinds would be more of an inconvenience than anything else. Now the lack of covering left the back door exposed and staring—a prying eye with no lid.

Charles turned out the dining room light. He turned off the light above the sink in the kitchen as well. There was nothing else that he could really do. The light was on outside and he had turned off most of the lights inside. That would obscure the view of anyone looking in.

There was still no proof that there had been anyone out there at all. Charles had a feeling in his gut. It had hit him out of nowhere that someone was there. Like being kicked by someone on a swing. First they weren't there and then swiftly and without warning, they were—with a vengeance. Was this all merely a side effect of his run-in with the red SUV? Was that why he was so spooked? It really didn't seem to be like him. He was not the nervous type yet there he was locking doors and turning out lights. Charles stood in the centre of the kitchen wondering what to do next. His panic on the deck had sobered him up. His joints were starting to ache as the alcoholic numb began to wear off. The main floor of the house was now dark other than the television. Charles walked to the front door and reached for the lock. He didn't know if the gang had taken a key when they had left for The Lampost. His fingers hesitated on the lock before letting go. This is idiotic, Charles thought. He was overtired and more than a little drunk. Sure, he might feel like anxiety had sobered him up but the fact was, it hadn't. The alcohol was still there coursing through his veins and making him jump to all sorts of irrational conclusions. That was it—it was the booze talking. Enough was enough. It was time to go to bed.

"Good night, Jamie." Charles said as he started up the stairs. Jamie offered no response. Charles hadn't expected one.

*   *   *

Charles awoke with a start. There was no way of knowing how long he had been asleep. He wasn't sure what had even wakened him. Were the others home? Had it been the heavy roll of the van's side door? He stood. He felt groggy. He didn't think he had been asleep for very long at all. He reached to the floor for his iPhone and looked at the screen—it was 2:00am. He hadn't been asleep for more than thirty minutes. Charles stood up in his *JAWS* t-shirt and NHL boxers and stretched. There was a full moon and it was bright. It shone in the window like a spotlight. Charles turned to the bedroom door and went downstairs. Jamie was wrapped in the blue neon glow of the television set. He didn't look up and Charles didn't say anything to him. Charles assumed that Jamie was asleep but it was hard to tell.

Charles walked into the kitchen and poured himself a glass of water from the tap. The ceramic tiles felt cool beneath his feet. He tilted his head back and drank, hoping that the water would help ease his inevitable hangover. He brought the glass down and his eyes focussed out the window. Charles held his breath as he watched a dark figure making its way across the backyard toward the house.

Charles didn't move. He didn't want to be seen. Any movement would attract attention to the kitchen window. He breathed through his mouth with shallow almost hollow breaths. His hands and his neck beaded

160

with sweat. Just before the strolling figure hit the back deck, Charles crouched down and headed for the living room. It was definitely a man, the figure had been too large to be a woman and its gait had been very masculine. Charles slipped around the corner and stood still. He listened. There was a light click and a rumble like distant thunder. He recognised it right away as the sliding glass door in the kitchen rolling on its track—so much for the lock on the door. Charles slid along the living room wall toward the front closet. Without looking, he found the doorknob with his right hand and turned it. The slatted shuttered door opened and Charles slid in, pressed against the coats and shoes. The doorknob released with a click like a starter pistol as far as Charles was concerned. It continued to echo through his head as he stood there in the musty darkness. He couldn't see so he closed his eyes and tried to listen over his own heartbeat. He needed to be so quiet. His heart, his lungs, his breathing, they all clamoured for top billing and he just needed everything to be silent and still. Someone had been watching him. He had probably been watching them all afternoon waiting for the right opportunity. Now, after seeing everyone else leave—he was in the house. Charles, Jamie, and a stranger were in the house.

The smell of the wood slats and leather shoes filled Charles' nose. The spacing between the slats was minimal. If the room were lit better, the stranger would be able to see the pink of Charles' face pressed behind the closet door without question. Charles squinted his eyes at level with a slat and tried to focus into the dark room. He could see movement. Slow, lumbering movement. The heavy thump of work boots filled the room. The intruder was too big to walk silently and he didn't bother trying. He walked up to the back of the couch and tilted his head down. Charles could tell that he was staring at Jamie. He stood there and stared. He didn't move. Jamie didn't move. Jamie was unconscious and unaware of the danger he was in. Charles had to squint to be sure that the two men were indeed motionless in the flicker of the television's blue light. With unexpected force and speed, the intruder thrust his hand down onto Jamie's head. Jamie began to flail. Muffled squeals bleated from the direction of the couch. Charles knew that the big man was smothering him. He had a large hand gripped over Jamie's mouth and nose and he was not letting go. Jamie clawed at the man with both hands but the big man didn't move at all. He didn't seem to even notice Jamie's hands grabbing at his coat sleeve, desperately trying to gain purchase on the man to throw him off balance. Jamie's legs danced in the air. Slowly losing strength and tempo. Finally, Jamie stopped moving all together. He lay limp; his lower body seemed to be pouring onto the floor. Even from the closet Charles could smell urine and faeces. The big man did not let go right away. He kept the same position. Holding Jamie down to be sure that his job was done, that he had accomplished what he had set out to do. After what seemed to be an eternity, the man stood erect but still stared at his handy work. Jamie was dead. The big man turned and walked out of the house the same way he came in, closing the sliding glass door behind him.

Charles didn't move. He stood frozen in the closet, unable to move. If he moved he was sure that his body would crack, fall apart like a shattering ice sculpture. His muscles still ached from his accident and now they were frozen from fear. His breathing was shallow. His heart still beat loud in his chest. That's all he heard—breathing and beating—the sound of his own blood. Then he became aware of another sound. It was close. Charles listened carefully until he recognised the sound. He wasn't sure what it was at first because he hadn't heard it in a very long time, not since he was a little boy—Charles was crying.

14

Charles sat in the backseat of Laurie's police cruiser with both hands wrapped around a steaming cup of coffee. He hadn't tried to drink it yet. He just sat holding it, taking comfort from the warmth in his hands. The heat travelled into his hands and up to his wrists before the cold of the night air got hold of him again. There was a blanket over his shoulders but his arms were exposed and they were cold. Charles could have adjusted the blanket but he didn't. He just sat there motionless and focussed on his cup of coffee. If he just focussed on the coffee maybe, if only for a minute, everything else would go away. There wouldn't be police lights flashing on the cruisers surrounding him; there wouldn't be cops yelling directives back and forth; there wouldn't be Brooke crying on the porch.

164

Most of all, emergency workers wouldn't be hauling Jamie's body into the back of an ambulance in a black body bag. There would just be Charles—Charles and Charles' coffee.

"Charles, I'm going to run you down to the hospital and get a doctor to look you over," Laurie said.

"I don't need a doctor," Charles said quietly although he wasn't sure that was true. He hadn't realised that Laurie was even sitting beside him. That couldn't be a good sign. Maybe she just got there, he didn't have a clue.

"I think we should get you checked out, babe." Laurie tried to sound sympathetic yet authoritative. It was a tone that Charles had heard Laurie use with great effect on civilians in the past; he had always thought it to be one of her strengths. This time was different. There was a chink in her armour. Charles could hear the tremble of fear underneath.

Charles sat quietly for a minute, then two. Finally he said, "I don't think I could take it. Even the thought of the bright hospital lights makes me want to throw up. I don't want people to talk to me. I just want to go home. Take me home, Laurie...please? Take me home and stay with me. If you still want me to go to the hospital in the morning, I promise I'll go just don't make me go tonight. Okay?"

Laurie got out of the backseat and walked over to Jeff. They talked briefly and she returned to the car.

This time, when she got in, she got in the front seat. Charles heard the engine turn over and the two of them drove off through Oak Bluffs toward East Chop.

The trees were enough to draw Charles' attention away from his coffee cup. He found nature calming, soothing. He got lost watching the leafy shadows and listening to the hum of the engine. It wasn't long before they were driving past the harbour. Sailboats clanged in their slips, tucked in for the night, and beyond them the black swells of the Atlantic Ocean rolled slowly.

Laurie parked her cruiser in the driveway of her oceanfront home. She got out of the car and went around to help Charles. When Laurie opened the door, Charles was struck by the smell of the sea air. He turned and put both feet on the ground and pushed himself up. He didn't have his cane. Charles decided that it must still be on the back deck of the other house. Laurie reached out her hand and Charles took it. From their position in the driveway, the house was just a black silhouette in the moonlight. Together they made their way up to the front door.

Charles stepped out of his flip-flops in the front hall—he didn't even remember putting them on—and made his way into the den off the kitchen. He sat down on the overstuffed couch and stared out at the ocean.

Laurie walked into the kitchen and turned on the light over the stove. She opened the fridge and pulled out a bottle of Kim Crawford Sauvignon Blanc. She poured herself a hefty glass, paused, and then looked over to Charles. "You want one?" she asked.

Charles nodded slowly. "Oh yeah," he said.

Laurie poured him a glass not quite as big as hers and brought it over to him. "I'm going to go upstairs and get changed. I'll just be a minute." She set her glass down on the coffee table and left the room.

Charles looked out over the ocean and sipped his wine. It was good. He heard the water running upstairs and knew that Laurie was taking a shower. He knew she would. Laurie could never change her clothes without taking a shower. Even when they were kids she couldn't change without a shower. The consistency pleased him. His mind dragged him back into the past, memories of him and Laurie as children. Not so much because Charles enjoyed reminiscing but rather because he was avoiding thinking about the present.

It was ironic, he thought. They were there on Martha's Vineyard to get married. He couldn't remember a point when he was happier. Certainly he had never been happier with his relationship with Laurie—it had never been stronger. That was exactly how every couple should feel on the verge of wedlock; however, this was also a low point for them. Charles could not remember a time when there had been more stress between them. The death of Sam Grover had been sad but someone had tried to mow down Charles in broad daylight and now someone had murdered one of their wedding guests right in front of Charles. There had been nothing that Charles could have done. If he had interfered, in his physical condition, there was a very good chance that he would be dead too. If Charles had rushed him from the closet he might have knocked the big man off balance but he would have toppled too. It would not have taken long for the big man to realise how injured Charles was and how to take advantage of that. One heavy-booted kick to the ribs or knee or head and that would have been the end of Charles. That didn't make him feel any better though. Charles had stood there frozen with fear in the closet and watched his friend die—that's all there was to it.

Charles had felt unsettled all evening. He had felt eyes on him when he was cleaning up the kitchen. It had seemed irrational at the time but now in hindsight, it did not seem irrational at all. More than likely, the big man had been watching all night, possibly all day. It was the same thought that Charles had about being followed by the man in the red truck. He must have been followed all morning prior to the assault.

Was the assailant in the truck and the man who killed Jamie the same person? Was the big man under the impression that he had just killed Charles, not Jamie?

Charles felt bile rise in the back of his throat. Cold sweat broke out across his brow. So not only had Charles not stopped the big man from killing Jamie, he had been the cause as well—if he was right. It made sense though. This wasn't a goddamn *Friday the 13th* movie where *Jason* was just picking off vacationers one by one. Someone had tried to take out Charles that morning and someone had succeeded in murdering Jamie that night. There was absolutely no reason for anyone to think that Charles wasn't home alone. Anyone watching the house would have seen Charles and only Charles wave his friends into the taxi. They would also have seen Charles cleaning up the kitchen and the back deck alone and then turn out the lights. There would be no reason to know that Jamie even existed. Once the big man had broken in to the house and found a man of the correct height and size in the dark asleep on the couch, there would be no reason to think that it was anyone but Charles. That was it. He had no proof yet but Charles knew he was right.

Laurie came down the stairs in her brown Lululemon tracksuit. She walked in to the den and took a generous mouthful of her Kim Crawford. She set the glass back down and returned to the kitchen. Charles watched as she reached down into the drawer in the stove and pulled out a tart tin and two bread tins.

"What kind of bread do you want?" Laurie asked. "I'm making a dozen butter tarts and one loaf of cheese bread. What do you want the second loaf to be?"

"Whole wheat?" Charles suggested.

"Done," Laurie said. She turned to the cupboards above the stove and began pulling down glass containers of flour, sugar, and other baking ingredients.

"I think Jamie was killed by mistake. I think that the big man was after me." Charles watched Laurie as he spoke. She stopped what she was doing and looked up at him. There was no colour in her face.

"I thought of that in the shower," Laurie said. She took a deep breath and exhaled. "It's a sobering thought."

"Yes but it's the only one that makes sense," said Charles.

"I agree. What's sobering is that he got within a couple of feet of achieving his goal and we still don't know why he's trying to kill you in the first place!" Laurie continued to measure out ingredients.

"So, that's where we start," said Charles. "If we're going to figure out who killed Jamie, we're going to have to figure out who wants me dead...and why."

"Agreed." Laurie rolled out the dough for the butter tarts.

"You know, on the outside it would seem like a dream come true to have a wife who bakes when she's stressed but the reality is that I'm going to be as big as a house." Charles forced a smile.

"I'm sorry Charles—I'm not in a laughing mood right now," Laurie said without looking up.

Charles let it go. He wasn't in a laughing mood either. He was trying to talk; he was trying to achieve some semblance of normalcy when nothing was normal at all. He left Laurie to her baking and walked out to the back deck.

The waves on East Chop were short at night. They lapped at the beach with black water and white froth. Charles' eyes followed the path of moonlight across the onyx ocean top as far as it went until the ocean and the sky blended together in the night. Charles took a sip of his wine and stared out to sea. He was trying to find the furthest point on the ocean that he could see. He felt like he was pushing his eyes out of their sockets with sheer will power. Pushing them out to see further. Somewhere out there was the line between ocean and sky. Things didn't go away. Things didn't vanish. People stopped looking for them.

Charles had already decided that the murder of Jamie and his attack on the street were related. It was the only way any of it made any sense; however, as much as it made sense that those two things were connected, it still didn't make sense that they occurred at all. If he removed them from the picture—the picture being his time on Martha's Vineyard—what was he left with? A wedding? Was there someone who didn't want Charles and Laurie to be married? A man had killed Jamie so Charles would assume that the connection would be to Laurie not to Charles. Laurie's ex-husband was dead. Who else wouldn't want them to be married? Charles didn't think that a jealous lover quite fit the mould and as they say, if it's not gelling it's not aspic. So what if he removed the wedding from that same picture? What was he left with then? He was left with Sam Grover—that's what he was left with.

Sam Grover had crashed his grandmother's car in front of Charles' vacation home and within forty-eight hours, both Sam and Jamie were dead. What if Charles was right and Jamie had been killed by accident? Let's say that the big man had gotten it right and that Sam and Charles—the only two people who were out at the car wreck that night—were now dead. Maybe following up on the attack on Charles wasn't going back far enough maybe they needed to follow up on Sam Grover. Why had Sam had the accident on Pond View Drive and more importantly why had he driven his car over the Gay Head cliffs?

Charles watched a shooting star fall out of the night sky toward the horizon. Charles was sure that he could see the horizon now—black on black.

The back door opened and Charles could smell the fresh clean of Laurie as she stepped on to the deck behind him. Charles lifted his left arm and she snuggled in close.

"The butter tarts are in the oven," Laurie said. "Don't let me miss the timer."

"Okay," Charles said. "Feel better?"

172

She looked up at him and smiled. "Much." She refilled his wine glass and then poured the remainder of the bottle into her own glass. "I'm sorry I snapped. This has not been a good night."

"No... No it hasn't."

"I think the real start isn't your attack but rather Sam Grover," Laurie said.

"I was thinking the same thing," Charles agreed.

"Good. Then the first thing we have to do is look at the autopsy report from Boston. Jeff should get it by tomorrow." Laurie took a mouthful of wine. "I want to know why he went over that cliff."

"Me too." Charles watched another shooting star. "Did you make bread too?"

"Yes. It's rising." Laurie watched the shooting star head for the horizon. "I'll be up for a while. You can go on to bed if you like."

Charles smiled at her. "I'm not tired."

"Me either."

"Are you cold?" Charles stared at her closely. Even in the moonlight he could see how blue her eyes were. He kissed her quickly. There was wine on her lips.

"I was but I'm not anymore," said Laurie.

Charles took her wine glass from her and set both glasses down on the wood table. "How long until your timer goes off?"

"Twenty minutes," Laurie said.

15

Charles woke up to the aroma of fresh brewed coffee mixed with fresh bread wafting in the open door of Laurie's bedroom. He had no idea what time it was. The sun was high judging by the light coming in the windows. Charles wasn't usually one for sleeping in but he certainly needed his rest after the last twenty-four hours. He was fed up—enough was enough. Playing the victim was not his shtick. The best defence is a good offense or something like that. Charles didn't want to waste anymore time feeling sorry for himself—he didn't want to waste anymore time thinking in clichés either for that matter—it was time to find out who was behind all of this before someone else got hurt...or worse. Last night he had come to the conclusion that the place to start was with Sam Grover's autopsy report. Laurie had figured there was a good chance that the report would come in today—tomorrow at the latest—and he wanted to get down to the police station as soon as possible to check it out. Charles remembered that Jeff had gone to talk to Violet Beacham yesterday as well. Learning what she had to say would be very useful in getting some insight into the life of her grandson.

Charles sat up faster than his body would have liked. He was stiff from his injuries and unusually long sleep. He moaned aloud as his back pulled in retaliation and his legs cramped. The pain was bright in his eyes making them water but Charles stayed upright, waiting for his body to adjust to his demands. The large glasses of wine were what had made it possible to make love with Laurie on the back deck the night before, he realised that now. He had needed that. Sometimes you just needed to get drunk and fool around—a wise woman said that once... a wise woman indeed. That closeness, that intimacy reminded him why he was there in the first place. It pushed the grisly goings on out of his mind at least for a moment. He knew that Laurie felt the same way. Their touch and warmth told them that these horrors were not the norm; it told them that life was beautiful on Martha's Vineyard—they just needed to get through this. It had worked like a charm.

Gingerly, Charles swung his legs out of the bed and put his feet on the floor. He remembered trying to stand in the hospital and took it extra slow. He didn't have the cane that the doctor had given him either. It had been left behind at the rental house. That house was a crime scene now. Charles realised that he had no idea where his friends had all slept last night. They couldn't have stayed there. Charles was sure that even if they had been allowed, at the very least, Claire wouldn't have wanted to sleep under the same roof where Jamie had been smothered. Charles stood up. He felt wobbly for a second or two but all in all not bad—just stiff. He was sure that some of that coffee he could smell would straighten him out quite a bit.

Charles limped into the kitchen, straight toward the coffeemaker. Laurie had left a mug out for him in front of the machine. It was a Starbucks City Mug from Toronto. He had mailed it to her as part of a birthday present a little over a year ago. He always used it when he was on the island; transversely, when he was in Toronto, he always used a mug from the ArtCliff Diner or The Black Dog. Charles filled the mug to the three quarter mark and then took the milk out of the fridge to top it up.

Charles could see Laurie sitting on a wooden Adirondack chair on the back deck. She was wrapped in a throw blanket and drinking a coffee of her own. Charles grabbed two butter tarts from a plate atop the kitchen island and made his way out to see her.

Laurie turned her head at the sound of the opening of the back door. "Good morning... How are you feeling?"

"Not bad—all things considered," he said. Charles passed Laurie a butter tart and she reached out from under the blanket and took it. "What about you? Did you get much if any sleep?"

"Some," she said with a mouthful of sugar, butter, and pastry. "Enough."

"These tarts are fantastic!" Charles stared at the half a tart still in his hand. His mouth was suddenly awake with the perfect combination of overwhelming sweetness and a sting of salt. "So many people miss the point with butter tarts. That bite of saltiness is the key to the whole thing."

"It's your Grandma's recipe," Laurie stated smugly.

"She'd be proud of you," Charles said.

"I couldn't ask for much more than that. I miss my Grammy...and your Grandma. They were both amazing ladies." Laurie stared out at the ocean. The wind had the waves a little higher than they had been the night before. The sun sparkled a path right toward her across the water. It was so inviting and warm she almost felt she could run across it.

"We still have Nana—my dad's mom and your dad's mom is still alive...isn't she?"

"Yes," Laurie said as she rinsed the last bits of butter tart out of her mouth with her coffee. "I don't get to see her much anymore. I'm on Martha's Vineyard and she's in Newfoundland. She can't travel for any number of reasons and me...this stupid job..." Laurie trailed off.

"Hey! What's the matter here?" Charles began to get up from his own chair to kneel beside her but his knee and hip resisted so he thought better of it. He reached out for her hand instead. "This isn't like you."

Laurie took his hand. "Isn't it? I've been a blubbering mess ever since you got here. At least that's the way it seems to me! First the wedding, then you get attacked by someone in a truck and now—*now*—one of our wedding guests has been murdered by someone who probably thought that he was killing you—the man I'm supposed to be marrying this weekend!"

"What do you mean supposed to be marrying? Aren't you still marrying me, Laurie?" Charles' eyes widened.

"Are you serious? Of course I'm marrying you but I don't see how we can do it this weekend! How can we?" Laurie said.

"We can because that was our plan. That was why our friends have made the trip. Some have flown in from another continent! Yes, there is a lunatic out there trying to destroy or end our lives and I for one am not going to give him the power or the satisfaction of doing
178

so!" Charles was adamant. "We can't let him, Laurie. We absolutely cannot! We have to get married as planned. Let's just catch the son of a bitch and wrap up this investigation by then."

Laurie looked at him with watery eyes. "Charles, are you sure?"

"One hundred per cent," he said.

"Oh shit! That's the doorbell!" Laurie leapt up from her chair, grabbed the coffee mugs, and took off into the house. A couple of minutes later, she returned with fresh coffee and Chief Jefferies.

"Jeff!" Charles said.

"Good morning!" Jeff said. "How are you feeling? You look stronger than you should considering what you've been through."

"I'm feeling pretty good actually," Charles said. "Jeff, what happened to my friends who were staying at the Pond View house?"

"We took them all over to The Edgartown Inn. A couple of the guys had to double up because it wasn't entirely empty yet but half of it was for your wedding. It all worked out pretty good. The state will pay to put them up for a couple of days. Edie will make some extra cash and they get a great place to sleep."

"Best place on the island in my book," said Charles. "Thanks for getting them settled, buddy."

"No problem at all." Jeff leaned against the cedar railing and set down a manila envelope beside him using his coffee mug to hold it in place. Once sure that the wind would have no effect on it, he sank his teeth into a butter tart. "Good God! These are awesome!"

"Thanks. Is that why you're here Jeff? You knew I was stressed out so you knew I'd be baking?" Laurie looked up at him shielding her eyes from the sun to see his face.

"Well, the three of us needed to talk and I thought it would be nicer to talk here than at the office...where there would be no fresh baked goods." Jeff grinned. "I would have been pissed on my way here if I passed you on the street!"

"What did you want to see us about?" asked Laurie.

"This envelope," Jeff said. He held his tart in his teeth and pulled the envelope out from under his coffee mug. He passed it to Laurie.

"What is it?" asked Charles. Charles watched Laurie pull the contents out of the envelope.

"It's Sam Grover's autopsy report!" she exclaimed.

"They faxed it in from Boston early this morning," said Jeff. "It must be a slow day on the mainland. That's all I can say."

Laurie furrowed her brow as she read the report.

"Well?" asked Charles. "What's it say?"

Laurie passed the report and the envelope to Charles. "Very interesting," was all she said. "On the surface, it looks like he died from contusions from the car crash but a lot of these are not consistent with the crash. There are a lot of contusions here. The coroner has marked every one of them down and I've never seen anyone banged up like this merely from a crash—especially someone who was wearing his seat belt, and Sam was." Laurie kept reading. "Tox screen found cocaine and strychnine in his blood."

As soon as Charles saw the white forms, he remembered that they were the same forms he had seen two years ago when he had been on the Vineyard. That autopsy had been for Karl Bass—the man who had been shot and fed to a shark at JAWSfest. Same standard white medical form but filled in with very different grisly details.

Charles read quietly while Laurie and Jeff watched in silence. He read the last line out loud, "Cause of death was asphyxiation."

"It seems that Sam Grover wasn't very selective about where he got his cocaine," said Laurie.

"Do you think so?" Charles asked.

"Charles, his body was full of cocaine and strychnine," Laurie said.

"Yeah, I don't understand the strychnine." Jeff asked. "I thought it was rat poison."

"Jeff, a dealer will sometimes cut cocaine with strychnine to bulk it up, make it go that much further to make that much more profit," Laurie said.

Jeff shook his head. "I've heard of talc, baby formula, even creatine but strychnine? Jesus Christ..." Jeff grimaced.

"This is a really high concentration of strychnine. That did not build up over time; that was an extreme dose." Charles looked back at the autopsy sheet and ran over the coroner's notes with his finger. "Look at the number of contusions—he seized pretty badly. No wonder he lost control of the vehicle and drove over those cliffs. Look at the hyperthermia and the rhabdomyolysis! To present these symptoms I think he was dosed."

"So you think Sam Grover was murdered too?" Laurie asked.

"I do now—unless it was suicide but that would be a pretty horrible way to commit suicide. Strychnine acts as an antagonist to glycine and acetylcholine receptors—"

"Can you speak English?" Laurie asked frustrated.

"Sorry. Strychnine prevents the chemical in the body that controls nerve signals to the muscles from doing its job. Those chemicals work like the muscles' off switch. When they don't work correctly, muscles have severe painful spasms. Eventually the muscles tire and the person can't breathe. The victim literally suffocates in his or her own body. I think the worst thing is that they are conscious for the entire experience. Doesn't sound like suicide."

"I see your point," Laurie said. Her face was pensive. "By the time cocaine hits the street though, it has been cut several times by each dealer who handles it. It's usually only about twenty or thirty per cent pure. They'll cut it with anything they can get their hands on to increase their profit margin."

"Yes but in order to have levels that high in his blood, the last batch of cocaine would have to have a particularly high level of strychnine in it. I mean a level that any experienced cocaine user would notice at the point of purchase, don't you think?" asked Charles.

"You mean he wouldn't have bought it if it had that much strychnine in it?" asked Jeff.

"I doubt it," said Charles.

"So, it was cut into his cocaine after the point of purchase? Why?" Jeff said.

"I don't know yet but there was enough strychnine in his system that he would have had a seizure behind the wheel," Charles said. "A seizure in such a tight space..."

"That would certainly explain all of these contusions. It looks like he was tossed in a burlap sack and beaten with a baseball bat!" Laurie said.

"I guess that does explain why he drove himself off the cliffs." Jeff shook his head. "Someone wanted it to look like an accident. I totally doubt that Sam would have cut his own stash with more strychnine—that doesn't make sense."

"So Jamie was the second murder," Charles said. "Sam Grover was the first."

"So it would seem," Laurie said. "I wonder if that will make Violet Beacham feel better or worse?"

"Oh! Jeff! How did it go with Violet Beacham yesterday? You went to see her after you dropped me off, didn't you?" Charles looked at his friend eagerly.

"It never happened," Jeff said.

"Why not?" asked Laurie.

"She cancelled. She said that she wasn't feeling quite up to snuff. She rescheduled for today at the same time." Jeff took a mouthful of coffee. "It's still on as far as I know. Charles, why don't you come with me? I'd say that all three of us should go but I have a feeling that she might find that a little overwhelming. Besides, she hates your guts, Laurie."

"It's mutual." Laurie rolled her eyes.

"No kidding," Jeff said. "Anyway, having Charles there kinda makes sense. He was at both accidents. He might be able to help. Also, he's not an authority figure. If he's overly polite, he might actually help put her at ease. He'll diffuse the officiousness if you know what I mean."

"Charles, do you feel up to it?" asked Laurie?

"Oh, I wouldn't miss it," Charles said. "Just give me a few minutes to clean up."

184

"Whoa! It's not until four o'clock this afternoon, bud," Jeff said.

"Oh, right—sorry." Charles said. "Laurie when does that bread come out of the oven?"

Laurie shook her head in disbelief. "It should be ready now. Jeff, do you want some bacon and eggs and toast made out of freshly baked cheese bread?"

"Lord love a duck! I'm in! I'll come in and make some more coffee too," said Jeff.

"I'm just going to sit here—I'm wounded." Charles grinned.

"Enjoy it while it lasts." Laurie kissed him on the head as she walked into the house.

16

With Charles in the passenger seat, Chief Jefferies turned his cruiser from Lake Avenue onto Seaview Avenue. Harthaven began just past the sea wall that marked the end of The Inkwell Beach.

Charles looked out the window, across the driver and over the steering wheel and the dashboard, toward the ocean. The weather was turning. Clouds rolled in, blocking out the summer sun that had warmed them on the deck that morning. Winds pushed the waves of the Atlantic with a new strength. Each wave crashed against the shore a little harder and a little louder than the one that preceded it.

"I didn't see this coming," said Charles.

Jeff followed Charles' gaze toward the sea. "I did," he said. "The wind is always a dead giveaway. Wind is always a sign that change is coming."

"That makes sense," Charles mused. "Do you have an agenda that you want followed with Violet?"

"Not a strict one. I'll let her lead," Jeff said. "Violet is the type who will have a lot to say. There are some people who make you pull everything out of them like teeth—Violet is not one of those people." Jeff kept his eyes on the road as he spoke. "You saw her the other day. If I know Violet, she will have rehearsed this interview as more of a one-woman show. She'll think we should sit there, listen, and be grateful, then go home." Chief Jefferies slowed the car as it began to rain. "It will be up to us to get her to elaborate where she doesn't want to elaborate and we'll have to do it without asking her any direct questions. That would be rude—at least Violet will think it's rude. That's where you come in..."

"Me? What am I going to do?" Charles asked.

"Just be yourself," Jeff said. "You'll be perfect." He turned briefly and smiled at Charles.

"Alright... I'm good at that."

"How are you feeling?" asked Jeff.

"How do you mean?"

"Well, you've been beaten up pretty badly and a lot of crap has gone down. You must have a lot on your mind."

Charles sighed. "I'm more worried about Laurie than anything else—truth be told."

"That's a pretty cool thing to say," Jeff said. "It's really cool actually."

"Is it? Why?" Charles asked. Charles could think of a number of reasons why it might be considered a good answer but he was curious what Jeff's reasons were.

"If something shitty were to happen to Chris and me, I wouldn't want him to worry about me exactly but I'd be happy if I found out that he did. You know what I mean? Also, if Laurie is the first thing on your mind, then your body must be healing. You must be in less pain."

"You know, you've really changed since I first met you Jeff," Charles said.

"Really?" Jeff was surprised. "What makes you say that?"

"I'm not sure how to say this without sounding really condescending," Charles laughed. "Maybe I shouldn't have brought it up."

"Just say it." Jeff grinned.

"Well, you have really grown up!" Charles blushed. "I really feel completely obnoxious saying that!"

"No need! I'll take it as a compliment. I probably have grown up since you met me. When I met you I was—"

"Jack Burrell," Charles interjected.

"Exactly," Jeff nodded. "I was Jack Burrell. A lot of things have happened since we met—I got married, I became chief of police. Those things are bound to change anybody."

"That's true." Charles nodded.

Jeff turned the car to the right putting the Atlantic Ocean behind them. The rain was light but it was enough to intensify the green of the trees like steaming vegetables. They weren't far up the road when Jeff pulled the car over and put it in park.

"Here we are," Jeff said.

Charles looked out the window at the grey cedar, two-storey home. It was a handsome home, well maintained and manicured—that didn't surprise Charles. Violet Beacham was definitely the *keeping up with the Joneses* type. What struck Charles was the house looked old. It really needed some TLC, thought Charles. There was no way Violet would be able to do the maintenance herself. Violet was an old woman and her days of painting windowsills on the second storey or cleaning and fixing the eaves trough were far behind her. Those would probably have been her grandson's chores. Charles' chest felt heavy. The more he learned about Violet Beacham, the more he pitied her.

Charles stepped out of the car and stood stiffly in the spitting rain. The weather made the grey house look a little sad, Charles thought.

"Hello there!"

Charles turned in the direction of a voice he did not recognise.

"Hi Mr Phillips!" said Jeff.

"Chief, I've told you before—please call me Craig. You make me feel like an old man." Craig Phillips hopped down from the back of a large rental truck. He pulled off one work glove and extended his hand. Jeff shook it. "Who's your friend?" Craig asked looking at Jeff.

"Craig, I'd like you to meet Charles Williams. He's—"

"I know exactly who Mr Williams is. I'm pleased to finally put a face to the name!" Craig began to walk around the squad car. Charles met him halfway.

"It's Charles."

"Thank you, I'm Craig." He extended his hand and when Charles took it, Craig shook it firmly.

"Why do you know who I am?" asked Charles.

Craig shrugged. "It's a small island; you're marrying a police chief. That's usually enough around here." A hearty laugh boomed out from behind neatly trimmed grey moustache and beard.

"Well hopefully you haven't heard anything too terrible," said Charles.

"I've been an islander all my life, Charles. You get pretty good at filtering out the bullshit." He lowered his voice and nodded toward the Beacham house. "You two will be here to see Violet I suppose."

"Yes sir," said Jeff. "That reminds me—how long will your moving truck be here Craig?"

"She was in to see you about that, wasn't she? God love her—she's a pistol! I heard about that too. Cynthia baked her up some Danishes by way of an apology. Violet wasn't too fussy on the apple but the prune did the trick!"

"Talk about filtering out the shit..." Charles said.

Craig Phillips roared with laughter. "You said it not me!" Craig choked his laughter down. "Really, we shouldn't laugh. I know the old girl is a handful but she just lost the only family she had. That's a tragedy, that is." Craig straightened up with a newly sombre expression. "That's going to take a lot of the wind out of her sails—you mark my words."

"You're probably right," said Jeff. "Anyway, we'd better go in and see her. It was nice to see you again Craig. Give my love to Cynthia."

"You know I will. Always a pleasure, Chief," Craig said. "Good to meet you, Charles. Congratulations on your wedding."

"Thanks very much."

Jeff came around the car to meet Charles and the two men made their way up Violet Beacham's front walk. Large drops of water rolled off the leaves of the overhanging oak tree. Charles found it ironic that they were getting wetter under the tree than when they were standing directly in the rain. When the stone walk came to an end, the two men found themselves at the front door. The three front steps nestled tightly under a white wooden trellis. The front door and the screen door were also wood painted white. Jeff rang the doorbell and the two men waited in silence for Violet to answer the door.

When the door opened, it opened slowly and heavily like the metal door of a bank vault. The dark of the room paired with the sheen from the wet screen door made it almost impossible to see the person who stood there. Slowly Charles was able to make out the silhouette of a small woman. Not because she had come forward but rather because his eyes adjusted. It was Violet Beacham.

Violet Beacham stood stoically in the doorframe but Charles could see that this Violet was different. Where once had been ramrod-straight posture—her shoulders now sagged. Where her eyes once burned with fire—they greyed with ash and black coal. She tried to maintain the exterior for which she was famous, but it was gone. Charles expected it was gone for good.

"Chief Jefferies," Violet spoke with a noticeable absence of emotion. "Thank you for coming." She looked Charles over from head to toe. "I wasn't expecting there to be anyone with you. Do you really feel that it's appropriate that I should have to discuss the personal details of the loss of my grandson in front of a total stranger?"

Charles tried to muster a sympathetic but subtle smile. It was impossible to figure out what she was thinking. She had made no effort to reach for the screen door; perhaps she wasn't going to let them in at all.

"Mrs Beacham, this is Charles Williams. He was with your Samuel at the first crash in Oak Bluffs and then on-site at Gay Head. I have asked him here to fill in some blanks wherever possible both for your own personal interest and for my investigation." Jeff spoke in the same tone one would use in a job application.

"Your investigation..." Violet pursed her lips. The first emotion she expressed since they got there was not a positive one.

"Mrs Beacham, he tried to save your Samuel..." Jeff continued. "I thought you might want to talk to him."

Through the beads of rainwater jewelling the screen door, Charles saw Violet Beacham's expression soften. She reached out for the brass knob of the heavy door. She did it smoothly but Charles was sure that she did it to steady herself. "Well, you'd better come in then hadn't you?" Violet stepped back into the dim of the vestibule to make way for the two men. "Chief, close the door behind you please."

"Yes, ma'am," Jeff said.

Charles and Jeff pulled off their shoes and padded down the hall after Violet. There was a natural light emanating from the next room but it left the corridor very dark. Once in the living room—the source of the light—Charles paused to take it in.

The room was painted in off-white and trimmed with dark stained wood. The dark wood flooring peeked out from underneath elaborate and multi-coloured oriental rugs. Two cream coloured sofas faced each other in the centre of the room each with their own vineyard-themed throw cushions. A stone fireplace took up one entire wall and settled in as the focal point of the room. The stones were large and varied in shape. It was the kind of fireplace that had once been used to heat the house two or three hundred years ago. Overall, it was the décor of a warm and inviting room not cold and austere, as Charles had anticipated.

"Have a seat, gentlemen. I'll be right back with some tea," Violet said.

"Oh please don't go to any trouble on our account, Mrs Beacham," Jeff said. Charles and Jeff sat facing each other on the couches.

"I always have tea at four o'clock, Chief Jefferies. It's already steeping. I just have to collect it."

"Would you like some help?" Jeff asked.

"No thank you. You can bury me in a pine box on the day I can't collect my own tea," Violet said.

194

When the door to the kitchen closed behind her, Jeff leaned in close to Charles. "Not all of the wind has left her sails," he said quietly.

"Clearly!" Charles said.

Violet returned with a tray burdened with a delicate teapot with matching china cups and saucers and a plate of two apple Danishes and one prune Danish. "Please leave the prune Danish for me but by all means, you help yourselves to the apple," she said as she set the tray on the coffee table. Violet sat down on the wingback chair between the sofas and facing the fireplace. The hearth served up a crackling blaze, the heat from which could be felt from their seats six feet away. "That Cynthia Phillips makes a lovely pastry, I'll give her that. I think the key is that she uses her own homemade preserves for the fruit. I know she only brought the Danishes because their truck is blocking my view but it was very kind of her to bake them just the same. She could have just as easily bought doughnuts from The Black Dog or Back Door Donuts."

"Would you like me to pour the tea, Mrs Beacham?" Jeff offered.

"That would be fine," said Violet. "There's milk and sugar and there's lemon."

Jeff looked at Charles. "Would you like milk or lemon?"

"Milk please," Charles answered.

Jeff reached for the creamer but before he poured, Charles stopped him. "Pour the tea first please, Jeff."

Jeff looked at him quizzically but set down the creamer, reached for the teapot, and began to pour.

Violet turned her gaze to Charles and studied him carefully. Feeling her studying him, Charles turned to see the hint of a smile on her lips. "Tell me, Mr Williams, who are your people?"

"My family is from Canada, ma'am. I live in Toronto. I will be moving to your lovely island in the very near future. I'm marrying Chief Laurie Knickles."

The slight smile left Violet's face. "I see. Well, congratulations I suppose."

"Thank you, ma'am."

Violet turned her attentions to Jeff. "Chief Jefferies, I imagine you must have questions about my Samuel."

"Yes, I do. Is there anything that you can tell me about his recent health?"

"His health was fine. Samuel was an athletic boy." Violet took a sip of her tea. "Unfortunately, he had a couple of car wrecks. They happen all the time. I think you are making too much of this." She took a bite of Danish.

"Did you know any of Samuel's friends?" asked Jeff.

"No, I did not. Samuel was out most of the time but he did not share his plans with me. I loved my grandson very much but I'm afraid he was not very fond of me."

Jeff's expression was one of sympathy. "I'm sorry to hear that, Mrs Beacham."

Violet's complexion greyed and she drooped noticeably. "It was probably my fault, not the boy's. My daughter, Carla—Samuel's mother—left me a long time ago and never came back. I suppose I didn't do right by her either. Samuel never forgave me for that. Carla didn't know how to be a mother. One day she was gone and she left her child behind. The irony in that is she left him with me. Carla didn't know how to raise him because I didn't know how to teach her. She should have given Samuel up for adoption, everyone would have been better off...Samuel would have been alive at least."

"Did she leave by herself?" asked Jeff.

"No, she left with Samuel's father. They were both young and stupid."

"What was his name?"

"Louis. Samuel's father's name was Louis. The man didn't have any family—wasn't even an islander." Violet shook her head with disgust. "Not that I'm in any position; I did no better."

"Mrs Beacham, this might not be my place but I think that growing up in a house with someone who loves him is a good start. Not every child gets that," Charles said. He was afraid that he had overstepped his boundaries as soon as he said it.

"You're right, Mr Williams, it's not your place," Violet said weakly. "But I appreciate the sentiment just the same."

"Mrs Beacham, the coroner's exam showed that Samuel was a habitual drug user. Did you know about that?"

"No." Violet flushed and straightened in her chair.

"Judging by the report, he had been using for quite some time," Jeff said. "I really don't mean to upset you by this but it's important that we contact anyone Samuel may have talked to in the last few days. Now—"

"Chief Jefferies, I think I'm going to have to ask you to leave now. I'm going to have to lie down. This has been extremely difficult and I am not a young woman!" Violet leaned forward to set down her cup and saucer. She misjudged the distance and the china hit the tray with a sharp crash. Tea slopped out of her cup and onto the table but Violet made no effort to clean it up. She fell back into her chair looking more worn than Charles had ever seen another human being look. Her chest heaved under her dark blue housedress.

"I'll get that," Jeff said reaching down to mop up the tea.

"Leave it!" snapped Violet. She took a deep breath and the fire that had burned in her belly when Charles met her returned. "Chief Jefferies, my Samuel did not use cocaine. If I find out that you've been spreading any such salacious filth, I will sue you and the Oak Bluffs Police Department for slander. Now please, see yourselves out." Her inner light extinguished once again and she sank back into the armchair.

"I'm sorry I've upset you, Mrs Beacham—I assure you that was not my intention. I will be back with a warrant tomorrow to search Samuel's room and personal effects. Get some rest now."

"It was a pleasure to meet you Mrs Beacham," said Charles.

"It's always nice to meet a well-brought-up young man, Mr Williams."

Charles caught a bewildered side-glance from Jeff as they turned to leave. At the doorway to the living room, Charles looked back at their hostess. Violet's eyes were closed and her head tilted back to rest on the high back of the chair. Her mouth hung open slightly. She looked dead.

It was still grey when they got outside but it had stopped raining. They walked to the car in silence.

"Chief Jefferies!" A feminine voice sung out from across the road. Jeff looked up and Charles turned around to find its source. "Chief Jefferies! Hold up a second would you?"

A beautiful woman in her early forties came out from behind the moving van in front of the Phillips' house.

"Mrs Phillips, what a nice surprise! What can I do for you?" asked Jeff.

Cynthia Phillips was an immaculately put together brunette. Her hands were well manicured and her clothes hung as only expensive clothes could. She walked across the street with an effortless and confident stride. In her hands was an opaque leftover container with a blue lid. "You can take these Danishes—that's what you can do for me. If I leave them in the kitchen, Craig will eat them all or worse—I will! Neither one of us needs that."

"That's very thoughtful of you, ma'am, but you don't have to do that."

"Chief, I'm forty-two not eighty-two. Call me Cynthia," she said. "Take the Danishes. I made two dozen but it's only the two of us here. I actually made them for Violet Beacham but she certainly doesn't need that many either. Take them to the police station, take them home to your handsome husband, just get them away from me!" Cynthia looked at Charles and smiling, handed him the container. "I'm Cynthia Phillips. You must be Charles Williams."

Charles smiled. "I must be."

"It's good to finally meet you." Cynthia smiled at Charles with a flirtatious grin. She stared him straight

200

in the eye and held it just a little too long before breaking away. "I've heard a lot of island talk about you."

"Yes, I get a lot of that," Charles said humbly.

Cynthia turned her attention back to Jeff. "How is Violet?"

"Beat," said Jeff. "Would it seem out of place for you to stop in to give her a hand? I wouldn't ask but I think she could use a hand—a woman's hand—to maybe clean up a bit and help her lie down or something. I don't think she has anyone here anymore."

Cynthia nodded. "Don't worry about a thing, Chief Jefferies. She still has my plate from taking her the Danish so I'll use that as an excuse to pop my head in. If I just go over to help, she'll turn me down flat—island pride and all of that."

"Thank you. I'll come around later to see how she's doing," said Jeff. Jeff pulled open his car door and Charles followed suit.

"It was a pleasure, Mr Williams, albeit a brief one," said Cynthia.

"Thank you. It was for me too," said Charles before slipping into the passenger seat.

Jeff turned the key in the ignition and slowly the car pulled away. After a quick wave, Cynthia Phillips strode up the walk to Violet Beacham's house.

"Where do you want to go?" asked Jeff.

"Would you take me to Edgartown?"

"Sure thing."

"Thank you," said Charles.

"Well, Violet Beacham sure liked you," Jeff said, driving back toward Seaview Avenue.

"You told me to be myself," Charles grinned. "I guess I'm more charming than you realised."

"I guess you are!" Jeff shook his head. "I've never seen anything like it—not when Violet Beacham is concerned anyway."

Charles chuckled. "She's okay, just a little sad and a lot scared. There's a new world coming in and taking over and she doesn't understand it. She keeps trying to fight it but she doesn't have much fight left in her, the poor old girl. So I tried to offer her some old-school manners. I guess it worked."

"What are you talking about?" Jeff furrowed his brow in bewilderment.

"The tea," said Charles.

"Oh yeah, what was that all about—tea before milk—who cares? It's all going to mix together and go down the same hole." Jeff shook his head.

"It's considered proper manners. Back in the day, fine bone china would not break if you put the hot tea in first; however, the cheaper sets did. Common people would pour the milk in first to cool the tea and save the cup. If you pour the milk first, you are implying that your hostess's china is poor quality."

202

Jeff turned his eyes from the road and gawked at his friend. "Where do you get this stuff?"

"Don't look at me like that—I didn't make it up. Blame the British," Charles said. "Anyway, I thought that Mrs Beacham would appreciate it."

"She sure did. Well played," said Jeff. "I can't believe all the stuff you've got rattling around in that brain of yours. Anyway, the visit was kind of a bust. We didn't learn anything. All we did was upset an old lady and learn that Cynthia Phillips makes a mean Danish." He shook his head.

"That's not exactly true," said Charles. "I think we learned a lot."

"How so?" Asked Jeff.

"You told her that Samuel used *drugs* and she insisted that she knew nothing about the *cocaine*," Charles said. "How did she know that we meant cocaine?"

"So she did know about the drugs!"

"She knew about the drugs," Charles said.

"I knew I brought you along for a reason!" Jeff beamed.

17

Charles walked up the stairs of The Edgartown Inn. The front porch was empty. It wasn't raining but the day was still damp, cloudy, and grey, and not made for lounging around outside. He opened the screen door and immediately saw his friends chatting in the library.

"Hey, everyone," said Charles. "How is everybody?"

Brooke got up from her place on the leather sofa and ran into Charles' arms. "Oh, luv! I've been worrying about you all day! This is just horrible! Poor Jamie. He was never any harm to anyone, was he? What's someone want to be doin' him in for?" Brooke's eyes began to water.

Charles hugged her but wasn't exactly sure what to say. He couldn't very well tell her that everything would be alright. It wouldn't. One of their group was dead. Nothing was going to change that. Charles hadn't really given himself time to think about it in depth emotionally. He just shut off that part of his brain. If he broke down then Laurie would break down and so would the rest of them. Once this was sorted out, once the perpetrator was apprehended, then he would pour himself a double scotch, go sit on the end of the pier at Laurie's house and let it all out. Until then...

"Come on, Brooke, pull yourself together." Kevin stepped up and took Brooke gently by the shoulders. "We just finished saying that we had to stay strong for Charles' sake, didn't we? Jamie would have wanted that. Jamie wouldn't have wanted us all running around upset. Hell, Jamie would want us all lying on the couch watching *JAWS*, wouldn't he?"

The group chuckled at the accuracy of Kevin's observation.

Brooke nodded. "I know. You're right. Just seeing our Charles made me start blubbing. I'm sorry."

Charles smiled. "That's okay. How is everyone making out here? I'm sure Edie is taking good care of you all, isn't she?"

"She sure is," said Brad. "This place is great. I've never been here before. This is where you stayed during JAWSfest?"

"Yes it is," Charles said. "I wouldn't recommend any other place on the island over this place. Did you all have breakfast here this morning?"

"We did—outside on the back patio. It's lovely out there," said Brooke. She managed a smile.

"I thought I heard your voice!"

Charles turned around to find Edie standing behind him.

"Charles, can I talk to you for a minute please?" Edie asked.

"Sure. Am I in trouble?" asked Charles.

"Aren't you always?" Edie led Charles down the heavily decorated hallway to the empty dining room of the inn. "Sit!" she said pulling out a chair.

Charles did as he was told and Edie sat down beside him.

"What's going on, Charles?" Edie asked.

"What do you mean?"

"*What do I mean?*" Edie exclaimed. "Charles, one of your wedding guests has been murdered! The bulk of your guests are now staying at my inn because your house is a crime scene. The wedding is supposed to be this weekend! Is it still on? I haven't heard from you or Laurie. I have only received a fragmented story from your friends. I've been worried sick!"

Charles felt his face flush. He was embarrassed. They had been so focussed on pursuing the investigation that neither Laurie nor he had thought of talking to Edie or his friends. They knew that they were safe at the inn and left it at that. "Oh, Edie, I'm sorry. I just didn't think."

"Damn right you didn't think!" Edie said. "Charles you should have called."

"You're right," Charles said sheepishly. "Edie we were so Hell-bent on getting the investigation over with so that everything could go back to normal that we forgot that we left some people drifting. Those guys in the library must be thinking the same thing. I've been a shit but it really wasn't done out of malice."

Edie smiled. "I know that, sweetie." She patted him on the cheek. "That's why I'm not killing you myself." Edie stood up and straightened her black cardigan. "Now, go talk to your friends. I know they're feeling a little stranded but promise me that at some point this afternoon, you and Laurie and I are going to have a talk."

"I promise," Charles said. He stood up and kissed Edie on the cheek.

"I'm just glad you're okay," she said. Edie spoke with a little more emotion than she had expected. Her voice cracked—it caught her off guard.

"I am," said Charles. "Don't worry about me."

"With your track record? I barely have time for anything else!"

"Nice," smirked Charles. "I guess I'd better go in and talk to those guys. I owe them an apology too."

"I would say so," Edie said. "So, I should continue planning your wedding then?"

"The show must go on," Charles smiled weakly. "I really don't want to give that bastard the satisfaction of knowing that he ruined our day. That just wouldn't be right."

"I see your point, my love, but if you haven't caught him yet and you stop your investigation to have a wedding—that wouldn't seem right either."

"I know. We'll get him." Charles patted Edie on the shoulder and then leaned in to kiss her on the cheek. "We'll get him."

Charles turned around and made his way back to the library. His friends were sitting exactly where he'd left them. They all looked up at him with expectant eyes. He realised then that what Edie said was true. None of them would say it; they all figured he was upset enough. He could see it in their faces though. Charles had left them at the scene of the murder with no explanation. Surely Jeff had told them something, hadn't he? Hadn't one of the officers on duty told them anything? It's possible that when this group had been whisked off to The Edgartown Inn, the police didn't know anything concrete and certainly would not have speculated or offered up any half-truths. In fact, Charles realised that there was a good chance that Jeff and Laurie wouldn't be too thrilled with him giving away too many details of the case without checking with them first. *Now what am I going to do?* He thought. I have to tell them something.

"You guys, I can't tell you how sorry I am. I left you last night without a word. Did the police tell you anything?" Charles asked.

"Well, you don't have to apologise. You didn't do anything wrong. You must have been just as upset if not more upset than we were!" Brad said. The group murmured in agreement. "We're not mad, we're just a little bit confused is all. What exactly happened? We took a cab home last night from The Lampost and found the place over-run by police. They told us that Jamie was dead—had been killed—and we had to move here to the inn. That was it."

Charles nodded his head solemnly. It was becoming harder and harder to block out his emotions about the loss of one of their group. He felt pressure building behind his sinuses and a glaze of moisture forming over his eyes. He fought it back. He inhaled deeply.

"Charles, you don't have to say anything if you don't want to but where were you when this all went down?" Brad asked. "Are you allowed to tell us?"

Charles thought about it. He wasn't giving up details of the murder. He couldn't see why he couldn't answer that question. "I was there," Charles said. "I had come downstairs after being asleep for a while—I'm not sure how long—not long. The house was dark and when I was standing in the kitchen, I saw a man coming across the backyard toward the back door."

Charles' audience was quiet. They barely breathed. "I'm not sure why I thought he was there to hurt anyone. It would have made more sense to think that it was a neighbour coming to use the phone or something along those lines. I had been jumpy all night. When I saw him, he scared me. I didn't know what to do so I panicked. I was so banged up that I certainly wouldn't have been able to fight him off. I ran and hid. I hid in the hall closet. The man came in and smothered Jamie while I watched." Charles could feel his face flush. The pressure started to build behind his sinuses once again and as hard as he tried to fight it, a tear ran down each cheek. He was quiet for some time; they all were. "Some friend, huh?"

"You can't blame yourself," said Tina.

"She's right," agreed Matthew. "You'd probably be dead too if you had tried to get in the way. That wouldn't have helped anyone."

"You did the only thing you could do," said Brad. "I can't believe you had to watch that. That's nightmarish." He shook his head. "Still, I don't understand why anyone would just come in and pick him off. I mean, who would want Jamie Ross dead?"

"I think Jamie died because the big man thought he was me," Charles said. He wasn't sure that he should elaborate on this point but it was too late now. "It ties in with the attack on me with the red truck. Don't you think?" That wasn't exactly the whole truth but it was good enough, thought Charles. He wasn't telling them anything they didn't already know. That would have to do for now.

"That's true," said Kevin. "So what are you going to do now?"

"I'm not sure. I'm going to walk over to the police station and see what Laurie is doing. She will probably have some ideas on how she wants to proceed. I'm sure that Chief Jefferies will want her input."

"You want to meet us for dinner later?" asked Brooke.

"Sure," Charles said. "Sand Bar?"

"Oh, I love the Sand Bar!" she said. "I need a few pints to get through all of this."

"Me too," said Matthew.

"Alright then, let's meet at Sand Bar at seven o'clock for drinks and then go next door for supper at Nancy's. Good?" asked Charles.

"Good," the group said in unison. It was clear that they were all still shaken from the events of the night before but the simple act of being together and planning an outing under a thin veneer of normalcy left each of them in a calm or a comfort that none of them had felt that morning.

Charles turned around. Standing just inside the front door was Craig Phillips.

"Hello again!" Craig said.

"Craig! This is a surprise," said Charles with a start. He hadn't heard Craig come in. "What brings you down this way?"

"Are you kidding? I'd walk all the way down Beach Road for one of Edie's breakfasts!" Craig smiled the same warm smile that he had given to Charles earlier that morning.

"I know what you mean," Charles agreed.

"Sorry to interrupt but Charles we're going to take off," Brad said.

"No problem," said Charles. "I'll see you tonight." Charles and Craig stepped out of the way to let the group file out of The Edgartown Inn. They watched as they went down the steps and turned toward the parking lot by the library.

"Would you join me?" asked Craig.

"Oh I appreciate that but I'm just heading out." Charles motioned toward his group of friends.

"Rain cheque then. That's okay—Edie's good company. I try to get down here once a week—between you and me, I think Cynthia's jealous! That reminds me—Cynthia was over to Violet's house after you left, and she said that Violet was pretty wound up when she got there. Cynthia talked her into lying down, and while she slept, Cynthia made her some soup. She said that after Violet woke up from her nap and got some soup into her, she was much better. Tell Jeff and Laurie for me would you?"

"I sure will," Charles said. "They'll be happy to hear it."

"I'm glad. You be careful on that leg. It's a long walk to the police station," Craig said.

"I will be," Charles left the inn and made his way down the steps cautiously. He headed down North Water Street. Maybe Craig was right, all of a sudden Peases Point Way seemed like a long walk.

*   *   *

Charles walked through downtown Edgartown lost in his own thoughts. His mind skittered from one subject to the next without catching anything. In the rental house, someone had murdered Jamie right in front of him. That someone could very well have been trying to kill Charles. On Beach Road someone had tried to kill Charles in his or her SUV, or at the very least scare him. Was it the same someone? Before any of that, Charles had run out into the night to help a man in a car accident who—not long after Charles had met him—killed himself by driving off the Gay Head cliffs. It had been a rocky week and all of this weighed awfully heavy on his plans to marry Laurie. Maybe Edie was right—maybe they should cancel the wedding but how could they? Friends had flown in from England! Laurie had arranged to take time off work. Charles didn't even live in the country yet! He was only there for a short time.

Charles thought about Violet Beacham. She was a sad old woman now with no family. Sam Grover had been her only grandson, her only blood relative. On that night, the night of the first car crash, Sam had mentioned his mother but Charles now knew that to be a fabrication. The desperate lies of a man trying to get away from the scene of a wreck caused by his own drug abuse. What it must have been like in that household. Neither Violet nor Sam seemed to be happy people at all. Charles had been in Violet's home and under normal circumstances it would have seemed warm and homey but inhabited by Violet and Sam, the house must have been cold and tense. Charles remembered that the room had been decorated pleasantly enough but when it all came down to it that just wasn't enough. It's the people, the family who lived in a house who made it a home. The Beacham house was a home of loss. It was sad.

Charles squinted as he focussed on his surroundings. He was on South Water Street. He had walked right by Main Street. He looked up at the sound of American flags flapping stoically not far above his head. He was not far from the Victorian Inn. He could see the famous Pagoda tree directly across the street from it. It was enormous. Its feathery leaves in full growth not yet ready for its late summer flower. Charles remembered reading that Captain Thomas Milton brought it over from China as a seedling and planted it in front of his house in 1837. It was now the largest Pagoda in North America. It absolutely blew Charles' mind that trees could be two hundred years old. How could Charles be looking at a tree that had been planted in the same year that Martin Van Buren was sworn in as the eighth president of the United States and that an eighteen-year-old Victoria was crowned Queen of the United Kingdom? It was truly awesome.

The rain began to fall again and Charles put up the hood of his yellow Black Dog rain slicker. If there was a better way to announce himself as a tourist on Martha's Vineyard than wearing Black Dog paraphernalia, Charles didn't know what it was. The rain began to fall harder. Instead of retracing his steps to Main Street and going up, Charles decided to go past the Pagoda, turn right at Davis Lane, and follow it up to Peases Point Way and the Edgartown Police Station. He quickened his pace but kept walking. His injuries prevented any real speed. Other people ran past him for cover but Charles did what he could manage. He would not have run just to get out of the rain anyway. There was something comfortable and cosy about a walk in the rain and it really was raining. The drops were coming hard and fast. Charles squinted reflexively from the splashing water. It was difficult to see. Charles turned right onto Davis Lane. On his right was the exterior of the Amity Police Station from *JAWS*. Charles smiled at that. When Steven Spielberg had shot that scene, it had been a bright and sunny day. The foliage had been a lot less rich. There was a trellis where Brody had walked through a small gate yelling, "Just have them fill out the form... just fill it out!" Charles stopped briefly in the pouring rain and stared at the fence, trees, and the gate, seeing *JAWS* in his head. A very big part of him wanted to just get lost, to pretend that everything was okay but it wasn't and— *BEEEEEEEEP!*

A car horn sounded not three feet behind him. Charles jumped and his knee twisted. He winced and screamed aloud as his weight returned to his injured leg. He hobbled out of the way and the car drove past him. Charles' heart pounded in his chest. He wasn't sure if it was the rain or the fact that he had been lost in his own thoughts but he hadn't heard the car at all. If the driver had come around the corner at any serious speed, Charles might have been hit. He reached out and grabbed hold of the lowest branch on the tree beside him. His breathing was still laboured. He raised a hand and held it out flat—he was shaking. Charles needed to pick up his pace. He wanted to see Laurie. When he saw her face, he would be fine. She wasn't far away.

Charles walked further down the lane. His leg hurt every time he put his foot down. Every time his heel hit the pavement, there was a sharp pain behind his knee. The rain fell heavier—a blue-grey curtain of water isolating him from the rest of the world. The sound of the rain pelting the trees and the pavement was like the amplified sizzle of bacon. Charles wiped away the droplets of water hanging from his eyelashes. He squinted just in time to see the red metal of the SUV heading straight for him.

There was nowhere to run. The lane was too narrow to evade the truck. Charles' knee wouldn't allow him to run or jump. The truck was aiming straight at him. It was twenty feet away at most. Charles dropped. He turned his head and pressed his eyes shut. He waited. The truck roared over him. The brakes screamed in Charles' ears. He was under the truck now. The heat from the car's undercarriage was burning his face. Charles opened his eyes as much as he dared. There was a click over top of him—a mechanical click. The driver of the SUV opened the door and stepped down. Charles could see a wet, black boot planting firmly onto the pavement and then another.

Charles shimmied away from the driver's side of the truck. He bent his knees reflexively and burned them against the hot metal. Charles bit his lip to stifle a cry. His injured legs were useless pressed into the ground away from the burning heat of the vehicle. His hands found as much purchase as they could on the wet gravel and he used them to pull himself sideways. Soon he found grass and he was at the side of the laneway. He grabbed a hedge trunk and pulled with all of his might. Once out from under the truck, he took one last look toward the driver's side—the driver was kneeling down surely for proof that he had been successful. Charles pulled himself face-first through the shrubs that outlined the backyard of a private home. Branches scratched his face, small sharp sticks pulled at his skin. Once his shoulders were through the hedge and over the mound of earth, he slid through easily. Charles got up to all fours and then stood on his good leg. His assailant could get though the hedge just as easily as Charles if not easier. Charles limped as quickly as he could through the backyard toward the side of the house. Briefly, Charles considered banging on the door of the home but if there was no one home, it was a stall that he couldn't afford. The driver of the truck could be right behind him. Charles wasn't breaking pace to find out. He wanted to get to a busy street and to the police station as soon as possible. Laurie was all he could think about.

Charles limped past two homes before he found another street. He wasn't sure which one it was. It was just as narrow as Davis Lane. He turned right and made his way up in the direction of Peases Point Way. The rain was still very heavy. Charles was sure that the truck and his assailant were long gone again. Had the

218

driver come across him by chance? Was he being followed? There was no way that the driver would be stupid enough to hit and miss and continue on the hunt.

Rainstorm or no rainstorm, this is downtown Edgartown for Christ's sake! thought Charles. This is downtown Edgartown! If he can come after me here, he can come after me anywhere.

Charles knew that Laurie would see it that way too. The grey shingles of the houses were almost black from the rain. The roses planted along white picket fences hung heavy with water. Charles crossed Summer Street and soon after, School Street. He had his bearings again. The pain in his leg was constant. He could feel the blood pumping through it. The skin was drum tight. Charles hoped that he hadn't done permanent damage.

At Peases Point Way, Charles could see the police station. He pushed the pain out of his mind and walked that much faster. At the station, he hopped up the stairs with his good leg. The front doors flew open and Charles ran in with all of the force he could muster.

"Oh my god! Charles!" Laurie ran out from behind the front desk and grabbed him with both arms. "Jack! Call an ambulance!"

Charles shook his head. "I don't need an ambulance. I'm okay. I probably look worse than I am."

"Jack, forget the ambulance—come give me a hand. Help me get him back into my office. Bring the first aid kit." Laurie wedged herself under Charles' left arm and Jack took the right. Together, they got him into a chair in Laurie's office. "Get his clothes off him, Jack."

Jack helped Charles out of his raincoat and his shirt. He was soaked all the way through to his skin. "Charles, if you can use your arms to push yourself up, I'll get your shorts off."

Charles nodded. "Don't you think you should at least buy me a drink first?"

Jack chuckled but Laurie did not.

"I'll go get him a blanket from the closet," Jack said.

"Thank you, Jack," said Laurie.

"Yes, thank you, Jack," Charles added.

Laurie looked at Charles sitting naked in her office chair. He was shivering, pale, and badly bruised. There were burns on his knees and face. His forearms and hair were smeared with mud.

Laurie knelt in front of him and gently dabbed at his burnt knees with an antiseptic wipe from the first aid kit.

"Charles, what happened to you?" Laurie asked.

"I got run over...literally," Charles said flatly.

Jack came back with a blanket, a washcloth, and a basin of warm water. "I thought you might want to wash up before we put fresh clothes on you. I assume your stuff is at the Chief's?"

Laurie took the basin of water and the washcloth. "Thank you, Jack."

"Yes, my stuff is all there," Charles said.

"Okay. I'm going to go get you some clothes. Give me twenty minutes." Jack closed the office door behind him.

Laurie looked at Charles. "He's good in a crisis. I'll give him that," she said. She reached out with a damp cloth and began to wipe his face. "Who ran you over and where?"

"Our friend in the red truck on Davis Lane."

"Jesus Christ," Laurie said. "If he can go after you there then you're not safe anywhere!"

"That's what I thought too." Charles winced as Laurie wiped delicately at his cheeks.

"Sorry," she said noting his discomfort.

"That's okay," Charles said. "Is it a burn? It was really hot under that truck. I'm sure my face was just millimetres from the exhaust pipe."

"No. It's not a burn; it's a scratch—a good one too."

"That would be from pulling myself through the bushes. I don't know what they were but they were sharp!"

"Clearly." Laurie finished cleaning his face and moved down to his knees. "Your knees are burnt.

They're going to blister—your left one is anyway..." She inspected closer. "...Maybe not the right."

"They're sore as hell. When I went to move out from under the truck, I bent them out of reflex and pressed them right into the truck."

"I'm sure. That wasn't the smartest thing to do." Laurie began to apply antiseptic to the burn.

"I'm sorry but I've never been run over before. Next time I'll be prepared!" Charles sat up straighter in the chair wrapped in the grey police blanket. "Jesus Christ, Laurie!"

"Why were you out walking by yourself, given everything that has happened to you so far on this trip?" Laurie's face was flushed. "I thought I told you to stay with other people? Is it too much to ask that you try and look after yourself until we get this sorted out? This is not a game, Charles! We already have two corpses—someone is trying to kill you!" Laurie's eyes began to stream with tears.

Charles tried to get up but his recent injuries told him not to. He pulled the other chair over beside him and patted the seat. "Come here."

Laurie took the seat and leaned in on his shoulder. "I don't think I can take much more of this," she said.

"Neither do I," agreed Charles. "I don't think you can take it mentally and let's face it, I can't take much more physically!" Charles forced a weak chuckle.

"That's not funny," Laurie said.

"I know."

Jack came back carrying an Edgartown Police T-shirt and track pants. "I think these will fit you," he said handing the clothing to Laurie. "They're leftover from the prizes we had from the picnic last year."

"Oh, good thinking, Jack!" said Laurie.

"Thanks Jack. They look comfy," said Charles.

"Look, the only way this is going to work is if you stay with me from now on." Laurie turned to face him straight on. "Don't you agree? Especially now, after you've been attacked in the middle of the day in Edgartown."

Charles nodded his head. "I agree."

"You do?" Laurie heaved a sigh of relief. "Well, at least that's something."

18

Laurie drove Charles out to her house on East Chop in silence. The sky was still grey but the rain had stopped. The police cruiser rolled to a halt in the driveway and Charles opened his door. Gingerly, he swung his legs out to the side and stood up. His left knee—his bad knee—was temporarily wrapped in a tensor. Laurie had debated in the station whether to leave it open for the burn or to wrap it for the swelling. They had decided to wrap it for transportation and then they'd remove it when he could properly elevate it in the house. Standing, Charles was glad they had wrapped it. His knee felt much stronger than it had all day. It felt stronger wrapped than it had with the cane.

Charles stood looking past the house at the ocean. There was sun cracking through the cloud cover at the horizon. Yellow beams of sunshine shot through the grey clouds like on an inspirational poster—the kind usually accompanied by a quote from the Bible. Charles did the math and figured that the sun was just less than four miles out and with the strong sea breeze that meant that the sunshine was on its way. That was definitely good news. He inhaled the sea air deep into his lungs. Charles felt a calm that he only seemed to feel when he was at Laurie's. He felt like he was home.

"It's funny but the sea breezes always seem stronger to me in the summer than in the winter," Laurie said. Charles didn't respond. "Charles? Are you okay?"

He turned to face her with a start. "Yes?"

"Are you alright?"

"I'm fine."

"Are you sure?"

"A hundred percent," Charles said, nodding reassuringly.

"Let's go in," Laurie said. She waited while Charles walked around the cruiser and then she placed her hand gently on his back. They walked in together.

The smells of wood, sea air, lavender, and home baking wrapped gently around them as they entered the front foyer. Charles pulled his shoes off with his feet leaving his runners still tied. Under normal circumstances, he would never do that. The fact that he had just done it was driving him crazy but with all of his injuries, it could not be helped.

"Why don't you go and sit in the den and I'll put on a pot of tea," Laurie suggested.

"Nothing stronger?" asked Charles raising an eyebrow.

"Don't tempt me!" Laurie said. "Technically, I'm still on duty and I'm also about to pump you full of painkillers. Sadly, I don't think wine or scotch is a good idea."

"Fair enough." Charles walked toward the back of the house. He turned back to make a quip but stopped short—Laurie was untying his shoelaces. He smiled warmly to himself and turned back toward the den.

Laurie walked into the kitchen and filled her kettle with water. She set it on the burner and turned on the stove. She caught Charles watching her mildly bemused. She shrugged, "I'm old school."

"So I see," Charles said. He leaned forward and threw a cushion on the coffee table. Gingerly, he propped up his leg and began to unwrap it. "Bring on the painkillers!"

"Take it easy, Charlie Sheen," Laurie joked. "I'm going to call Jeff, fill him in on the goings-on, and *then* we'll get you doped up."

"You're a regular Florence Nightingale," said Charles.

"Think Nurse Ratchet packing a gun." Laurie gave him an evil grin.

"...And handcuffs! Don't forget the handcuffs." Charles matched her evil grin for evil grin.

"Oh for Christ's sake!" Laurie shook her head. "I'm calling Jeff. I'll be right back."

Charles sat on the sofa looking out of the picture window. The sea breeze brought the ocean rolling in with a regular crash. The ribbon of sunlight breaking through the clouds that Charles saw earlier was closer and bigger. It wouldn't be long before the Vineyard was alight with sunshine. People were always happier in the sunshine. Problems didn't seem so insurmountable— most problems. Charles and Laurie still had to find out who had killed Jamie, who was trying to kill Charles, and now who had killed Sam Grover. Had the big man who killed Jamie also been responsible for the murder of Sam? It was too much of a coincidence for Charles to have Sam Grover in a car accident outside Charles' house, Jamie murdered inside Charles' house, and Sam Grover murdered all within a couple of days. Maybe that was it, thought Charles. The one and seemingly only thing that Sam and Jamie had in common—other than the fact that they were both dead—was Charles' rental house. So what was going on at the house?

"Jeff's on his way over here," Laurie said walking back into the kitchen.

"Why?" asked Charles.

"Well, if you were in better shape, you and I would be heading over to the Oak Bluffs police station and comparing notes with Jeff. I told him what happened to you and he wants to see you. He also agrees with me that you should be kept more or less under lock and key." The kettle started to whistle and Laurie took it off the burner. "Do you know how many of these I burn through because I never hear the whistle? I'm a fire hazard."

"Then get an electric kettle with an automatic shut-off like everyone else," Charles admonished.

"It's not the same."

"I'll buy you one."

"Fine. You buy me one, I'll use it." Laurie reached into the cupboard for rooibos tea and two mugs. She filled each mug and walked into the den to give one to Charles.

"I've been thinking," said Charles.

"Yes?"

"What do you see are the connections between Jamie and Sam?"

Laurie furrowed her brow. "I've been thinking about that too."

"Hello??" Jeff shouted from the front door.

"Come on in, Jeff. Do you want some tea?" Laurie called out. She turned and headed back into the kitchen.

"I'd love some! It's been a cold, damp day," Jeff said. He walked into the kitchen and took a steaming mug from Laurie.

"For some more than others!" Laurie pointed into the den. "He's in there."

Jeff turned toward Charles and did nothing to hide his shock. "Jesus! Talk about *rode hard all night, put away wet!*" Jeff headed into the den and sat down beside Charles on the sofa. "How are you feeling, buddy?"

"I'm alright. It could have been much worse," Charles said.

"I suppose that's true." Jeff looked over Charles' injuries. He grimaced. "Damn." He shook his head. "I think that we should keep you here under a twenty-four hour guard at least for a while."

"I agree," said Laurie.

"Well, I don't agree!" exclaimed Charles. "I'm the victim here! I don't want to be under house arrest!"

"Don't look at it that way," said Laurie. "It won't be forever. Right now you should be resting and healing. While you're doing that, Jeff is going to put a cop on guard here—that's all."

Charles knew that what she said made sense. "Alright. As long as it's only during my convalescence."

"Your conva-what?" Jeff asked.

"Then it's agreed," Laurie said. "Good. Let's get down to business. Jeff, we had just been thinking about what connections there were between Jamie Ross and Sam Grover." Laurie sat down in the club chair across from the sofa, facing Charles and Jeff.

"Sam was an islander. Jamie was not—he was from New York City. I don't know anything about Jamie at all. Charles, he was your friend. You must know something about him. He was here for your wedding after all."

"Not much actually," said Charles. "I met him through a *JAWS* Facebook page. He seemed cool enough; he knew everyone coming. He was actually coming more for the trip to the Vineyard than for the wedding. I invited him because he was here anyway—the more the merrier, you know?"

Jeff nodded.

"I actually meant what do the crimes have in common more than the individuals' histories. We can check them out easily enough," Laurie said. "Let's look at their deaths."

"Their deaths?" Jeff asked. "There's nothing in common with them at all. Am I missing something?"

"I see where you're going," said Charles.

"I don't," said Jeff. "Sam was in a car accident which you think was murder due to the high levels of strychnine in his system." Jeff took a sip of his tea and then he continued. "I buy that. That makes sense but Jamie was smothered in your living room, Charles. A man using a couch cushion smothered him. I suppose technically they both asphyxiated but the M.O. is as far off as it could possibly be."

"Agreed but what if Sam's death wasn't the first attempt on his life?" said Charles.

"Exactly," said Laurie.

"Did Sam say that someone had tried to kill him?" asked Jeff.

"No," said Charles. "But what if that car accident in front of my place wasn't an accident?"

Jeff listened intently.

"There was cocaine paraphernalia found in the wreck. Did you do a drug test on him after that first accident?"

"No—he refused. He demanded to see his lawyer right away and they posted his bail without us touching him. We have "implied consent" in Massachusetts but we don't have the legal right to give anyone a drug or alcohol screen if they don't want one. Most people don't know that."

"Well, I think we can operate under the assumption that he was under the influence. I saw him when he got out of that car—he wasn't making much sense and he was wired for sound. He certainly didn't want the police involved either."

"No—he didn't. Even still, that doesn't change the M.O. of either death. They don't have anything in common. The only thing that changes is..." Jeff stopped in mid-sentence.

Laurie and Charles looked at each other and back at Jeff.

"…Where it happened," Jeff said.

"Location…location…location," Charles said. "It's far too much of a coincidence for me that both men would have died at my house within a couple of days of each other."

"I don't buy it either. I don't know how that helps us exactly but figuring out that the two deaths are connected does make me feel like we're getting somewhere at least," said Laurie.

"You know," said Charles, "if we're going to continue under the assumption that the two deaths were connected because they both happened here, then they must also share one more connection."

"What's that?" asked Laurie.

"Me," said Charles. "It only makes sense."

"How do you figure?" asked Jeff.

"At the very least, someone has tried to do me some serious damage twice since I've been on this island. Sam rolled his car outside my house and I went out to save him. Jamie was murdered in the house when anyone watching would probably have thought that I was in the house alone. They probably thought that they were killing me." Charles smiled weakly but his heart wasn't in it and while he intended it to comfort his friends—it was clear that it hadn't.

Charles winced as he got to his feet. He limped over to the back window where he had a good view of the ocean. The sun was much closer than it had been. The cloud cover was being pushed away as he had predicted. The weather was so mercurial at that time of year. He watched the waves crash against the shore. "The summer breeze is so much stronger in the summer."

"Is it really?" asked Laurie. "I have always thought it was but I wasn't sure. I thought maybe it was just my imagination." Laurie got up and stood beside him in the window.

"No. It really is," said Charles.

"Why?" Jeff got up and stood with them watching the waves.

"Large temperature differences between land and ocean. That's why everything is always so changeable. You never know what's going to happen next," Charles said.

19

Charles sat on Laurie's overstuffed sofa in the den. He had been watching the ocean roll in for quite some time. Exactly how much time, he wasn't sure. Jeff had returned to the Oak Bluffs Police Station. Laurie was baking in the kitchen—banana bread by the smell of it, thought Charles. He could still see Laurie or more to the point, she could still see him, but she was engrossed in her flour, sugar, and mashed bananas, and seemed to be paying him no attention whatsoever. Having said that, Charles knew that if he even tried to get up from the couch she would be on him like a great white on a surfboard. So, he sat there with his leg up trying to sort and file all the information that he had accrued about this particular stay on Martha's Vineyard. Something that had happened since he walked off the ferry was the key to this whole mess and it was something that had happened at the rental house—he was sure of it.

When the doorbell rang, it jarred Charles out of his thoughts and back into the living room.

Laurie washed her hands quickly under the kitchen tap and dried them on her apron. It was a red and white apron in the pattern of the Canadian flag that Charles had mailed to her as part of her birthday present. Charles had intended it as sort of a joke gift but it actually looked quite cute on her.

"Hi! Come on in," Charles heard Laurie say by the front door. If there had been a response, Charles didn't hear it. A moment later, Laurie came around the corner with Jack Burrell in tow.

"Hi, Charles!" Jack said. "How are you feeling?"

"I'm not bad. Thanks, Jack." Charles looked toward Laurie quizzically but she refused to meet his gaze. Charles figured it out immediately—Jack was to be his babysitter. Charles began to heat up but quickly dismissed the emotion. He decided to go with it. There were a lot of upset people on the Vineyard at the moment and Laurie was one of them—the baking alone was telltale of that. Even Charles couldn't argue the fact that he needed to take it easy and Laurie was a good cop. It would be best if she went out and caught the person or persons behind all of this. Watching his every move and baking banana bread was a waste of her talents and certainly the root of many of her frustrations. Besides, she would only make the two of them fat. Charles loved banana bread... warm with a lot of butter.

"How's the knee? It looks pretty messed up," Jack said. "I remember once I was on my bike and it was raining, I went to take a turn too tight and I totally wiped out. I was on pavement and it totally took off all my skin on the side of my knee. I was pretty bruised up for a while. It was stiff too. I was really limping around for a while. The doctor gave me crutches but I didn't like them—they made my armpits hurt. It's a weird motion using crutches. Your body's not used to it. I think a cane is better, don't you—"

"Would you like to watch a movie, Jack?" Charles cut him off. He appreciated why Laurie wanted someone to keep an eye on him but Charles would rather run the Boston marathon than sit there all night listening to Jack's stream of consciousness. Running a marathon would be less exhausting too. Charles smiled to himself.

"Oh yeah! Good idea. I just got off work. I'd really like to watch a movie. Do you want me to call Giordano's and get a pizza?" asked Jack.

"Do they deliver?" asked Charles.

"No but I could go and pick it up," said Jack.

"Jack!" Laurie spoke sharply from the kitchen. "You're not leaving the house! I know that you and

Charles are friends but this is technically surveillance. If you can't handle it casually, I'll put you in a uniform and leave you outside the house in a squad car."

"I'm not sitting in here while Jack's outside in a squad car. There's no way," Charles said shaking his head.

Laurie slid her banana loaf into the oven and closed the oven door. Wiping her hands on her apron, she walked into the den where Charles and Jack were sitting. "I didn't figure you'd go for that but look, you've got to meet me halfway. I really need someone here—all the time—making sure that you are safe. I don't need someone running out for pizza or beer or porn and condoms!"

"I only said pizza!" Jack said innocently.

"You brought beer, porn, and condoms though right?" Charles deadpanned.

"What? No! What for?" Jack exclaimed.

"Some fun you are. Why'd you come at all?" Charles asked.

"Oh, Charles, shut up," Laurie said. "Jack—he's kidding."

Jack looked from Laurie to Charles and back again. "Oh! Oh you guys!"

"Alright? Just don't go out for pizza. Okay? You can order from Vineyard Pizza Place on Beach Road—they deliver," Laurie said. "No beer for either of you!" Laurie pointed at Charles. "You're on medication," she said and then turning her attentions to Jack she said, "and you're on duty!"

"I hope you're paying him for this then!" Charles huffed.

Laurie rolled her eyes at him. "Well I am now! Thank you very much."

"You were going to get him to do this for free?" Charles asked. "You're unbelievable."

"I was going to pay for his dinner!" Laurie said.

"I'm getting paid to eat free pizza and watch movies? Wicked pissah!" Jack exclaimed.

"Alright, I'm going upstairs to get changed and then I'm heading to work as soon as my banana bread comes out of the oven. You guys can have that for dessert. Keep the receipt from whatever you order for supper and bring it into work with you. I'll need it."

"Okay," Jack nodded.

Laurie turned to Charles. "How are you?"

"I'm fine. Go catch some bad guys so we can get married in peace...not in pieces."

Jack laughed.

"That wasn't funny," Laurie said.

"It was kinda funny," Charles grinned.

"I thought it was pretty good," said Jack.

"Jack, I'm dead serious, don't let him out of your sight. If he goes to the bathroom—go with him. You'd probably have to help him anyway," Laurie said.

"Okay," Jack nodded smiling.

"And if you need them, there's plenty of porn and condoms upstairs." Laurie winked, left the room, and headed upstairs.

"Sa-weet!" Charles said.

Jack laughed again... nervously this time.

*   *   *

"This is like the best scene in the whole movie. You have that great big dude in black with the big fancy sword doing all that fancy sword stuff and then Indy just shoots him. It's so awesome. You ever wonder how they come up with that stuff—those movie guys? They're wicked smart that's for sure," Jack said.

"It was an improvisation," said Charles. It turned out that Jack had never seen *Raiders Of The Lost Ark;* it was one of Charles' favourites. As soon as Laurie had left, they had popped it in.

"What do you mean?" asked Jack.

"It wasn't in the script. There was supposed to be a big elaborate stunt with the whip but Harrison couldn't get it together and he felt like crap—they all did—because the whole crew had food poisoning. He suggested to Spielberg that he just shoot him and Spielberg loved it," said Charles.

"Really? That's so cool!" Jack was amazed.

"Hollywood legend," Charles nodded.

"You're a lot of fun to watch movies with, Charles," Jack beamed with a hint of hero worship.

Charles laughed. "So are you, buddy." Charles looked past Jack into the kitchen. "Man, I could really go for a beer."

"Sorry, Charles, we can't. I'm on duty. That wasn't Laurie telling me not to drink that was the Chief of Police. Can't do it."

"I know it." Charles slumped back in his seat.

"Want more pizza or iced tea?" Jack offered.

"No, but I could go for some of that banana bread and some coffee. You can make coffee can't you, Jack?"

"Oh sure thing! I'm always the one who has to make the coffee at the station. The other guys make me do it because I'm the greenest cop but I really don't mind making it." Jack got up from his chair in the lounge and walked into the kitchen. "I like the smell of the coffee grounds and it sure makes people happy to have fresh coffee made all the time, I can tell you that!"

"I'm sure it does."

"I think I like it because it's a homey kinda thing. I spend a lot of time at work—especially now that Marcie's gone." Jack saw Charles wince at the name of his dead wife. "It's okay—I'm okay. You were there; you know what happened. I sometimes wonder how well I knew her. She was a really nice girl who got mixed up with the wrong people. I blame her father for that. I remember the girl I knew before all of that business with the Monster Shark Tournament. That girl—that's my Marcie. You know what I mean, Charles?"

"I know exactly what you mean," said Charles sincerely.

"Hey! I guess you do! You're about to get married yourself! We shouldn't be talking about my misfortunes! That's probably bad luck or something! You and the chief are really great! I'm glad that you're getting hitched. We all feel the same way down at the station—we were talking about it. I think the weather is going to be nice for you too! Did you see the sky? It's cleared right up! Look, I'll close the lights so you can see out back!"

Charles turned to face the back of the house and when Jack flicked the light switch, Charles could see the silhouette of a large man on the back deck pointing a gun at Charles' head. He dove for the floor. "Jack—get down!"

A single shot shattered a pane of glass in the French door.

Charles looked up from the floor to where the man had been standing. He was gone. Jack was right—it was a clear night, a cloudless sky lit by a full moon. Jack slid across the floor to Charles. "Are you alright?" he asked.

Charles nodded. "Yes, I'm fine."

"Stay here until I come back," Jack said. "Okay?"

Charles nodded in agreement. Charles was sure that the man he had watched kill Jamie was the same man he had just seen on the porch; Charles felt sure that it was also the same man who had tried to take him out with the red truck. Yes, Charles planned to stay on the floor exactly where he was. He wanted Jack to catch this man...by whatever means necessary.

Jack stood up and opened the back door. The deck was empty and grey. The door Jack opened was the same one the man had put a bullet through only a moment ago. All of the windowpanes reflected a fragment of the moonlight except the one that had shattered.

Charles pulled himself back up onto the sofa and then pulled up his leg. He sat there quietly in the dark and waited for Jack to return. He heard the front door open. Charles figured that Jack must have done a sweep—walked around the grounds. He was about to call out to him when Jack came back in the back door. Charles stared at Jack in the moonlight. He whispered, "Someone just came in the front door!"

Two shots fired in the dark. Jack hit the wall of the den as though he'd been kicked in the chest. He collapsed to the floor. Charles felt one bullet graze his ear.

"Jack!" Charles yelled. Jack did not respond. With all of his strength, Charles forced himself forward across the back room. When he got to Jack, he was unconscious. Charles shook him but Jack did not respond. Aware of movement behind him, Charles got up and headed out the back door. His bare feet padded across the shattered glass. Shards sliced deeply into his soles as he trod across them—each step stickier than the last. Charles knew he was bleeding but there was nothing he could do about it. If he stopped, he would be killed for sure. Was Jack dead? There was no way to know for sure. Charles limped onto the beach and waded past the shoreline. Charles had always been a strong swimmer. If he could tread water just off the beach, his assailant would not find him. He couldn't swim out after him. It would be impossible to see Charles against the black water but Charles would get a good look at the big man if he came out on the back deck. The salt water stung Charles' open wounds as he waded in but he figured that they were probably doing his wounds some good at the same time. Charles took his first breaststroke out into the sea, then another, then another. Thirty feet from shore he caught his breath, he almost turned around, what had he been thinking? In the mêlée, Charles hadn't thought about sharks—him of all people. His chest tightened and he began to panic. He was swimming by moonlight bleeding from his ear, his knees, and his bare feet. This was a terrible idea, he thought. He had to get out of the ocean. He turned to face the shore just in time to see the large bearded man step out of the back door. Now that Charles could see him standing in the moonlight, he knew with absolute certainty that it was the same man who had killed Jamie. Charles watched as the man crouched down to the deck and then reached out to touch something, he smelled his fingertips, and then stood again. Keeping his head down, the man walked to the stairs that Charles had taken to the beach. Charles may very well have left a trail across the deck but he wouldn't have left a trail in the sand—that was something anyway.

Charles thought he felt something against his foot. Was it panic? He needed to get out of the water. If he turned around, he was sure he would find a dorsal fin aiming directly for him; however, there was no way he could take his eyes off the big man with the beard either. Treading water, Charles started to move toward the edge of the property, toward the neighbours'. He didn't think they were on the island—he had seen neither hide nor hair of them. There was a thick brush between the two properties. At the very least, he could hide in there. Again—something feathered against his foot. Charles couldn't help himself; he splashed in panic and let out a slight yelp.

The big man turned quickly toward the ocean and stared directly out in the direction of Charles. Charles could not be sure of anything. Did the man see him? Was there something preparing to have him for dinner? Something swimming beneath directly beneath

244

him? Charles treaded water as slowly as he could. His arms moved as lightly as they could without letting him sink. The big man turned his head slowly from one side to the other. Clearly, he wasn't sure what he had heard or seen either. Charles continued toward the neighbours' property and the big man walked around to the front of the house looking for signs of a trail.

Charles slipped out of the water as quietly as he could. Water poured from his clothing and the night air was cold on his wet skin. As his wounded feet struggled to find purchase on the rocky beach of East Chop, there was an unnatural heave in the water behind him. He scrambled faster before turning not sure what to expect to be following him out of the ocean, but there was nothing. Charles sat on the rocks trying quietly to catch his breath. He stood slowly. The cold of the water felt good on his sore joints but still he was careful. He walked as quickly as he could, bent at the waist as if he were avoiding chopper blades. He hurried to the top of the bushes and stopped short. Heavy footsteps thumped the soft earth on the other side of the greenery. Charles braced himself in the bushes. If the big man with the beard came around the corner, Charles would have one chance to take him down with a heavy kick in the groin—one chance—but he didn't come around the corner. Instead, Charles heard that same mechanical click that he had heard lying under the truck in the rain. Charles sank onto all fours and peered across to Laurie's property. There he saw what he was hoping to see. It was right in front of him. Crawling out of Laurie's drive, onto the empty road, and eventually disappearing around the bend of East Chop Drive was a shiny red SUV.

20

"*Jesus H. Christ!*" Laurie yelled as she got out of her squad car. "*Charles? Charles?*" She ran toward the ambulance that was parked on her front lawn. She felt mild relief followed by guilt when she found Jack unconscious in the back on a stretcher. "Oh for Christ's sake. How is he, Marty?"

"He's not great," said the paramedic. "He took a bullet to the chest. They're prepping at the hospital. He'll need surgery. It's still lodged in there. Your boyfriend probably saved his life."

"Charles?" Laurie asked.

"Yep. He's inside." The paramedic reached out to pull the door closed. "We have to go."

"Oh sure. Thanks, Marty. Take good care of him. Keep me posted."

"You bet," said the paramedic.

Laurie stepped back as Marty swung the ambulance door closed. Laurie sprinted across the lawn, up her front steps, and went inside.

Charles was sitting exactly where she left him on the overstuffed sofa in the den. If not for the fact that he was getting his feet bandaged up, Laurie might not have known anything had happened—that and there was a throng of police officers in her kitchen eating her banana bread.

"I can't leave you alone for one goddamn minute!" Laurie exclaimed putting on a brave face.

Charles looked up at her. "You know what an attention-whore I am."

"Seriously? You're going to make jokes? Jack was just taken on a stretcher to the hospital where a surgeon is preparing to remove the bullet that is still lodged in his chest so naturally you figure I'm in the mood for witticisms." Laurie threw her car keys on the table and took a look at his freshly applied bandages.

"I'm sorry." Charles' face lost all traces of humour. "Did the paramedics say anything about Jack? All they would say to me was that they were doing all they could for him and that he would probably be fine."

Laurie shook her head before answering. "That's all they would tell me too."

"Oh," said Charles looking defeated.

248

"Well that's not entirely true. Marty—that's the paramedic—did say that you probably saved Jack's life. What's that all about?" Laurie fingered the bandage on Charles' ear. "What happened here?"

"Bullet grazed me," said Charles.

"Of course it did," said Laurie. "Jesus Christ, boy—the horseshoe that is wedged up your butt must be a doozy."

"It will take more than that to get rid of me."

"Clearly! Well, somebody's trying to figure out what it will take," said Laurie.

Charles sat and quietly took her in. He stared at her for a long time before speaking again. When he did, his words were carefully chosen and his voice was well measured. "I don't think that I could take it if Jack died because of me. That would do it. That would be too much for me."

"Okay, in the first place—Jack is going to be fine. Marty has prepared me for the worst before and he did not prepare me this time. Marty is the best. If he has every confidence that Jack will be fine, then I believe him. Second—and possibly even more importantly—none of this is because of you. *You have done nothing wrong.* You did not bring this on. There is at least one lunatic out there and only they are responsible—not you! So I want you to stow that shit right now. You got it?" Laurie looked him square in the eye. "I'm serious. *You got it?*"

"I got it." Charles nodded. "Oh! But I did learn something! It is one guy."

"Who is one guy?" asked Laurie.

"The man who attacked Jack and me today is the same guy who killed Jamie *and* it's the same guy who tried to kill me twice in the red SUV!" Charles was beaming with this last piece of information.

"How do you know that? We put out an APB on red SUV's but it was a joke! Do you know how many Jeeps and sports utility vehicles there are on this island? Almost every single islander drives one. We may as well have told people to be on the look out for fishing gear. There was no license plate and you didn't see the driver during either attack," asked Laurie.

"Well, I suppose that's true but today I did see the big man with the beard drive away in the same red truck."

"*Really?*" said Laurie. "So if we find that truck, we solve this whole thing."

"Yes ma'am," said Charles. "And we have to find it tomorrow."

"Why?"

"Because we're getting married the day after."

Laurie ran her fingers through her hair and rubbed her temples with her palms. "Charles do you still think we should?"

Charles nodded his head insistently. "Now more than ever."

250

"I suppose Jack would never let us hear the end of it if we postponed our wedding now. He never lets us hear the end of anything as it is." She chuckled a tired chuckle. "We can have the service in Jack's hospital room if you like—he would love that," Laurie smiled. "I'm not sure Dr Nevin would like it, though."

"Before we start making any radical decisions, let's find who's behind all of this and then see where we are. Okay?"

"Okay." Laurie nodded.

"You asked me once what I wanted for a wedding present—well, there you have it."

"What?" asked Laurie.

"I want a red SUV."

*   *   *

Charles and Laurie drove south on East Chop Drive listening to *Last Kind Words* by Rhiannon Giddens on MVYRadio. The blues guitar was the perfect accompaniment to the early morning sunshine singing across the East Chop between the Atlantic Ocean to the west and Crystal Lake to the east. Properties narrowed to impossible strips of land that barely accommodated the two-lane road, a split-rail fence, and the homes wedged upon them. Charles figured that there had probably been a lot more square footage when the homes were built but little by little, bit-by-bit, Mother

Nature was taking the island back to the sea. Charles was sure that there were a few storms every year, especially in the spring, that flooded this part of East Chop Drive completely and the houses right along with it but that certainly was not the case today.

Charles thought that as long as someone wasn't looking at him and his mass of bandages, a person would think it was another beautiful day on the vineyard—which of course, it was. At this very moment, the Vineyard was full of tourists, summer DINKS, and islanders. They were all going about their daily routines of shopping for souvenirs, eating lobster rolls, drinking Bad Martha's and Sam Adams, and swimming on State Beach and the Inkwell. They were eating at Nancy's Restaurant, drinking at The Sand Bar, and shopping at Slip77. There was well over a hundred thousand people on the island doing the things for which the island was famous; however, somewhere on Martha's Vineyard there was someone else operating insidiously amongst the vacationers. Someone cutting cocaine with strychnine and killing with it and now he had shot a cop and not just a cop—he shot Jack. Laurie and Charles drove south on the Chop. They were headed for the Martha's Vineyard Hospital.

"That's it," said Charles.

"What's it?" asked Laurie.

"If we've decided that the first attempt on Sam Grover's life was that accident outside my house on

Pondview and all of the attempts on my life have been by the same big man with the beard that I saw kill Jamie and shoot Jack, then he must think that I know something about that accident. He must be worried that I know something or I saw something that night!"

"Well did you?" Laurie asked. Her head turned back and forth between Charles and the road as she talked.

"I don't know!" Charles exclaimed.

"Well, you'd better think."

"Can we go back there?" asked Charles. "To the scene, I mean."

"I really want to go see Jack," said Laurie.

"So do I—I mean after that. Can we go there straight from the hospital?" asked Charles.

"Absolutely. We won't be long at the hospital anyway. Jack won't be up for much at this point. I doubt he'll even be awake. I just want to talk to the doctor and see how he's doing." Laurie patted the steering wheel reassuringly. "He'll be okay, Charles. Don't worry."

Charles knew that she wasn't talking to him and that was fine. Charles' mind was already back at the crash scene, back at that night. He started with the lights dancing across his bedroom ceiling and went from there. He tried to take himself through every detail. He had to remember if he was going to finish this.

The rest of East Chop went by in a blur as Charles' mind wandered. It wasn't until Laurie put the car in park that he came back to the present. His day trip to the night of Sam Grover's car crash had been for nothing. He didn't remember anything in particular that would make him a risk to anyone, certainly nothing that would be worth killing him over. Charles stared out of the windshield at The Martha's Vineyard Hospital. He was still as impressed by it as he had been the first time he saw it. That had been during what he now called The JAWSfest Murders—three years ago.

"Do you need a hand?" asked Laurie.

Charles shook his head. "I think I'm okay. Thanks."

Laurie stepped out of the car and straightened her uniform. Charles got out of the passenger side albeit a little slower than Laurie. They both closed their doors and started toward the main building.

"What about his mother?" asked Charles.

"Jack's mother?" asked Laurie.

"No, Sam Grover's mother," said Charles.

"I never met her," said Laurie. "Why?"

"Well, it's the one thing that I remember that stands out from that night that doesn't make any sense. I mean within the context of that night. Yes, he was in a car accident and yes, he was strung out on bad coke and strychnine—not your typical evening home at least not for most folks—but they're both at

254

least plausible. It's only the mention of his mother being sick that stands out as odd."

"Didn't we decide that he was full of shit? That he was lying to get away from you and the police?" asked Laurie.

"Yes we did but I was supposed to try and remember something that stood out from that night and that is what stands out. That's what is first and foremost in my head from that crash. Well, that's one of two things," Charles corrected.

"What's the other thing?"

"Remember when we were reviewing the scene the next day? He started running in the opposite direction that he had been driving. He kept saying that his mother was sick and then he ran off in the opposite direction." Charles stopped talking then to collect his thoughts.

The automatic doors slid open and Laurie and Charles stepped into the cool air-conditioned vestibule of the hospital.

"Hi, Chief Knickles!" The same plump and cheerful nurse was there every time Charles visited the hospital. She was there the first time he had visited regarding that boy, Casey, who had jumped off the JAWS Bridge onto the half-eaten corpse and she had been there when he had shown up to visit his friend, Mike, after Mike's brother had been shot.

"Hi, Connie, how's your day?"

"Better than yours, I imagine! You must be here about Jack? What am I sayin'? Of course you're here about Sergeant Burrell." Connie pressed a hand into her ample bosom. "Breaks my heart. You know I got a boy about his age—"

"Breaks my heart too, Connie. Where is he?" Laurie smiled politely.

"Oh—he's just down the hall on the left. I think you should be able to catch the doctor with him now if you hurry."

"Connie I don't really feel like hurrying. Would you page his doctor and have him meet me in Jack's room ASAP please? I sure would appreciate it."

"You bet, Chief." Connie smiled at Charles as they walked past her desk. A vague look of recognition and a half-smile crossed Connie's face when she looked at him. Charles could tell she was trying to place him but he offered no explanation. He got the distinct impression that Laurie didn't want to hang out and chat.

The door was open when they got to Jack's room but the doctor wasn't in it. Jack lay quietly in his hospital bed looking very much like a high school boy. His round face was completely void of stress marks or the wrinkles and the creases that come with age. He had good colour and looked quite comfortable. Charles had to admit that he thought Jack looked pretty good.

Chief Jefferies was asleep in the only chair at the foot of the bed. He jerked awake when Charles and Laurie walked in.

"Oh hey guys!" he said in a loud whisper.

"What are you doing here?" asked Charles.

"Jack's mother was here but I just sent her home for a shower and to get some breakfast. I told her I would stay with Jack until she got back. He's out cold. The operation went really well. He's going to be fine."

"Oh, thank God," said Charles.

"No kidding," added Laurie.

"Jack's mother was here all night. She needed a break but I knew she wouldn't leave him alone. I also knew you guys would be stopping by this morning so I told her I'd stay. Have you seen the doc yet?"

"No but Connie just paged him to meet me here." Laurie looked at her watch. "He should be along any minute. I'm surprised that Connie didn't tell me that you were here."

"I slipped in the other way. I'm not as good as deflecting her as you are. I get trapped at the desk and I can't get out!"

"I can see that," Charles chuckled.

"Chief Knickles. You had me paged. What can I do for you?" Charles, Laurie, and Jeff all turned on their heels like children hearing the approach of the principal.

"Dr Elkins, good morning! Charles, this is Dr Lureen Elkins. She works out of Boston General. When we need her, we are lucky enough to get her from time to time. Dr Elkins has a home in Vineyard Haven. Dr Elkins this is my fiancé—Charles Williams."

"A pleasure. Chief Knickles, I have already told your colleague everything that there is to know about Sergeant Burrell's condition."

"I'm sorry, Dr Elkins. I didn't know that Chief Jefferies was here and had already spoken with you. I wasn't expecting him," said Laurie.

"Without exaggeration, his surgery could not have gone better. He'll sleep for a while now. I imagine that he will wake up sometime tonight." Dr Elkins looked at her patient thoughtfully before continuing. "The bullet came out cleanly; it was the bullet of a .40 Glock. I'll have that for you to collect of course. It should be easy enough to trace. Difficulty is that it's by far the most popular gun on the Vineyard. The island is lousy with them, as you well know."

"It makes me feel better to talk to you directly just the same. Thank you for your time," Laurie spoke sincerely.

"That's fine. The hospital will call you as soon as Jack wakes up but as I said, I wouldn't expect to get that call before this evening."

"Thank you," Laurie repeated.

258

"I'll say good morning then," Dr Elkins left with her white lab coat flowing behind her.

Jeff turned to look at Laurie, "Where are you two headed now?"

"Back to the scene of the crime actually," Charles said.

"Which one?" Jeff asked.

"Pondview," Laurie said. "We think that the key to this whole thing has something to do with the accident at Pondview. At least Charles thinks so. I'm willing to give him the benefit of the doubt. What good is an I.Q. in the ninety-eighth percentile if you don't use it?"

"You sound like my parents all through high school," Charles said.

"I guess that makes sense. Do you know what you're looking for, Charles?" Jeff asked.

"Not a clue. I'm hoping I'll know it when I see it," said Charles.

"Well good luck," Jeff said. "Ninety-eighth percentile..." Jeff shook his head. "...Scooby-Doo makes better plans than that."

21

The rental property on Pondview showed no physical signs of change. The grass surrounding it was a patchwork of green and brown just as it had been the day he arrived. The house was well maintained—all of the shingles in good condition, the paint job looked relatively fresh. The bright greens and clean whites didn't look weather worn or faded. Still, there was something different about it. The warm welcome feeling that Charles had felt when he approached the house for the first time was gone and had been replaced with a sinister leer from every window. Charles was sure that he was projecting but that's how it felt to him. The police tape was still up but Charles knew that wasn't enough to make the house seem so foreboding. Flashes of Jamie's face being forced into the pillow, muffled choking sounds, the silhouette of the big man with the beard heading toward the house, and that feeling of hearing his own breathing against the closet door all spun around in his head like a macabre carousel. Charles felt mildly nauseous. He shivered.

"What's up?" Laurie had been watching him.

"Oh—nothing. Kind of creepy though, isn't it?" Charles forced a crooked smile but he wasn't sure Laurie bought it.

"It's just a house, Charles. Are you okay to do this?" Laurie walked over and took his hand.

Charles nodded. "Yes...I'm fine, really."

"Okay," said Laurie. "Do you want to stay out here? You probably don't have to go inside."

"No. I do. I have to start in my room and work my way through the entire night. At least, I think I do. That's the only way I can see this working."

"Alright, well let's go then," said Laurie.

They walked toward the house and Charles grabbed one of the wood posts when he stepped onto the porch. The cuts on the soles of his feet were shallow but sore. They were bandaged tightly for support and the bandages made them hard to bend. Charles felt like he was walking like C-3PO. Laurie pulled the police tape down from the door and typed a numeric code into the key box that hung from the doorknob. It popped open producing the key for the front door. Laurie inserted the key, twisted the knob, and the door swung open with ease.

The smell of the house hit Charles immediately. It wasn't a bad smell or a good smell but it was a singular smell. It was a combination of cleaning products and seasonal mustiness that Charles would always associate with that house and the events that had taken place in it—specifically witnessing the murder of Jamie Ross. All of the good times, the barbecue and the laughter of his friends, would forever stand in the wings behind the pounding tightness in his chest from that night. That would always be the one image that stood centre stage in his memories of the Pondview house.

Laurie stepped across the threshold and then stood back giving room to Charles. He stepped cautiously. Once both feet were inside, he looked straight up the staircase that led to the two upstairs bedrooms. He then turned to the right looking past Laurie at the living room behind her. She stood beside the closet where Charles had hidden from the big man with the beard.

Charles began to breathe heavily like he had that night. He was breathing through his mouth so as not to make a sound. His nose was full of the smells of wood and shoe leather just as it had been that night. He then remembered another smell, a darker, stronger smell. Jamie had lost control of his bowels in that room—

Charles had forgotten that until now. He continued to stare past Laurie, over her right shoulder into the room behind her; he saw the big man hunched over the couch staring at the limp body of Jamie Ross, who almost looked beheaded under the couch cushion that had been used to smother him. The big man straightened and turned to his left—away from Charles and the closet—and lumbered back in the direction from which he had come. The memories continued to come fast and hard. Charles could hear the heavy-booted steps that carried the man first through the kitchen and then out onto the deck. Once off the deck, there was no sound. Charles' memory was entirely back in the closet—his smells of wood and leather and faeces. Charles stood in the closet for a very long time, afraid to move, all of his muscles so tight that he thought he might shatter. Finally, he pushed forward with his body and fell out of the closet to the floor. The wood slat door collapsed under his weight. Slats splintered underneath him. On the floor, he gasped at the open air. He inhaled at the room like it was his first taste of oxygen. Released from the confining closet, the air was cool and fresh. Charles turned over and finding his balance on all fours, staggered to his feet. He didn't dare to turn on a light. What if the house was still being watched? He couldn't let the big man know that anyone else was in the house. Charles leaned over the back of the couch and pulled the cushion off Jamie's face but immediately wished he hadn't. Jamie's eyes were wide and dry from exposure. His mouth gaped unnaturally making Charles suspect his jaw was broken. His lips were pulled back over dry gums exposing at least three smashed teeth—the expression of terror on Jamie's face was fresh in Charles' mind now. He had pushed that memory out too. Charles would have been happy if he had never seen Jamie's unnaturally dry and faded eyes again but now he had and this time they would never go away.

"Charles?" Laurie asked in worry.

Charles looked at her and saw the concern in her face.

"Babe, you don't look so good," she said. "I think we should sit down for a minute."

"I'm not sitting down in here," said Charles still staring at the couch.

"No, of course not, go back out on the porch and sit in one of the rocking chairs. Okay?" she asked.

"Sure," Charles nodded. He turned around and sat on one of the two rocking chairs to the left of the front door. Laurie sat beside him in the other.

"Maybe this was a bad idea," said Laurie.

"Quite the contrary," said Charles. "I'm remembering a tonne that I had forgotten or blocked out or whatever you want to call it."

"Really?" asked Laurie. "That explains why you look like you've just seen a ghost."

"That's what it feels like."

"I didn't know what the hell was going on," Laurie shook her head.

"That night, I called you?" asked Charles. "I remember going for the phone in the kitchen."

"You called 9-1-1."

"Right," Charles said. "I remember now." Charles stared out into the trees that made up the barrier between the road and the front lawn. He thought about running out past it that night that Sam Grover had overturned his car. Charles needed to go over that night if they were going to get anywhere. "I'm okay now."

"Are you sure Charles?" asked Laurie.

"Yes I am," Charles said, standing up. "I want to get this over with."

"Alright, let's go."

Charles found his footing and walked back into the house. Laurie followed him. He purposely did not look back into the living room but rather walked directly up the stairs to the bedroom that he shared with Brad. Once in the room, he stopped and looked around briefly before walking across the blue carpet and sitting on the twin bed that had been his.

Laurie stayed in the doorway and watched him. "Anything?" she asked.

"No," Charles said. "Let me think about it. I feel like a psychic trying to read a haunted house."

"What's that feel like exactly?" Laurie asked.

"It feels stupid."

"That's what I was afraid of. I'm going to go back downstairs. I think I'm getting in the way, okay?"

Charles nodded.

"Let me know if you need me," Laurie said before turning and walking back down the stairs.

Charles sat in the quiet of the bedroom and looked around the room. He really did feel stupid. There was nothing in this room except a couple of T-shirts that Brad had left behind and Charles' bathing suit, nothing of any consequence. Charles lay back on his bed and thought back to that night. He had been asleep before the lights brought him to semi-consciousness, followed by the crash that jarred him fully awake. He remembered red lights and white lights swirling across the ceiling before the crash. He had then leapt out of bed and ran down the stairs. Today, there would be no leaping and running. Charles got to his feet and walked toward the stairs. He braced himself on the banister and made his way down slowly. It was easier than he thought it would be. Back outside, he walked across the porch and down the driveway toward Pondview Drive. He turned to his left— the same direction he had turned in search of Sam Grover's overturned vehicle. Charles remembered seeing the burning taillight in the blackness. It was the only thing that he had to lead him into the darkness.

He followed it, running into nothing—he tripped. No, he stepped on something. It had been heavy. Whatever he stepped on, it hadn't budged. A tree root maybe? It must have been a tree root. He remembered hitting something hard with his fist when he tripped. That would have been the tree. Charles turned around and looked back toward Laurie in the mouth of the drive. He felt a bit confused—disoriented. When Charles left the driveway, he headed in the direction of the crash site. That would have to be where he would have seen the taillight of the car. Even in the dark, he would have run in a straight line directly toward it. That's the only thing that made any sense. The taillight was the only thing he was able to see that night. There would have been no room for distractions. If that was the case, how could he have stepped on a tree root?

"What's the matter?" Laurie called out.

Charles beckoned her over with a hand motion and she jogged up to his side.

"What?" she asked.

"When I left the drive, just now, I headed directly toward the crash. That must also be exactly what I did that night. Wouldn't you think?" asked Charles.

"That only makes sense," Laurie agreed.

"Well, that night, I tripped. I tripped on something big. Up until now, I assumed I had tripped on a tree root. You know, a big one like at the base of a tree. I even hit something with my fist when I swung out to regain my balance. I thought it was the tree."

"But how could you have hit a tree if—" she started.

"—if I'm standing in the middle of the road?" he finished. "Exactly."

"So, what did you hit?" Laurie asked.

"I don't think I hit a what. I think I hit a who," said Charles.

"You think the big man with the beard was out here that night?" asked Laurie.

"What if he was?" Charles asked. "What if he caused the accident?"

"Wouldn't Sam Grover have mentioned him then? That would have left him in the clear," Laurie countered.

"Sam might have thought he killed him," said Charles.

"So why would he have killed Sam a day later?" asked Laurie.

Charles shook his head. "I don't know."

Laurie didn't say anything but waited for Charles to continue.

"The more I think about it though the more I think I hit a man and not a tree and if not him then who?"

"So, let's say it was him. Where does that get us?"

268

"You're right. It's all supposition at this point," Charles said sourly. He looked toward the crash site. Taking a deep breath, he continued in that direction. There were still long black skid marks down the centre of the road like a macabre treasure trail. Charles followed them past the Haliburton house on his left up to the turn where Sam left the road. Branches were broken, bark torn from tree trunks and the green matted and pressed where the car had ground to a halt.

Charles stepped down off the broken asphalt onto the forest floor and walked in until he was standing where the car had been. He remembered faded light from the car's interior and not much else. Charles' feet were sore from walking. He limped over to a freshly snapped tree and sat on the horizontal trunk. It felt good to take the weight off. Charles leaned forward and cupped his face in his palms. He rested his elbows on his knees. His eyes slowly scanned the forest floor in front of him—broken trees, pressed leaves, snapped passion flowers, an empty bottle of vodka, and a piece of paper...an envelope. Charles manoeuvred onto his knees and reached forward for the envelope. It was addressed but there was no stamp. It was addressed to Adam Haliburton—the same man that Laurie and Charles had delivered mail to the other day. This letter had been lying in the cool, wet muck for a couple of days. It was disintegrating on the corner and the seal was unglued almost halfway across the top. Charles scanned the horizon for Laurie. She was pretty far away. He looked back down at the envelope. Using his thumb and his forefinger, Charles popped the envelope open and peered in the top. There were two square plastic bags inside with something written across the front of them—he couldn't read them. He shook the envelope until the bags slipped down toward the open end; he then tipped the envelope and shook hard until one of the bags fell in his lap.

"What are you doing?"

Charles looked up to see Laurie looking down on him from the road. "I don't want to touch it. Do you have gloves?"

Laurie stepped down off the road and pulled a pair of latex gloves out of her shirt pocket. "Mail tampering is a federal offense."

"I didn't tamper with anything—I promise," assured Charles. "Not exactly."

Laurie looked at him disapprovingly as she put on the gloves.

"Look, the envelope was already deteriorating and open. I shook out contents that would have fallen out anyway," Charles said.

"We'll sort out the ethics later. What have you found?" Laurie reached down and picked up the bag from Charles' lap.

In her hand was a clear plastic re-sealable bag that held what looked to be a small amount of white powder. It was stamped with a stamp of block letters and the black silhouette of a shark. The letters read *WHITE SHARK*.

"*WHITE SHARK*—that's their brand? Everybody's got to have a brand now. It's amazing the amount of marketing that goes into the drug industry these days," Laurie said.

"Another name for an actual white shark is White Death—ironic," said Charles.

"Drug dealers—clever aren't they? Aren't they funny?" Laurie mocked gravely. Laurie held out her hand and Charles passed her the envelope.

"Not really," Charles said. His tone did nothing to hide his disgust. "We must have missed this envelope in our first sweep."

"It certainly looks like it but that doesn't seem likely. My team was out here for a long time and they're good. They would have covered every inch of this place. If that wasn't enough, you and I were out here right afterward. I hate to think that we would miss something as obvious as an envelope," Laurie said. "Where was it exactly?"

Charles pointed to the spot under the lip of the pavement where he found it.

"Doesn't that seem a little obvious to you?" Laurie asked.

"Yes it does," Charles said. "It doesn't matter though. There's still only one thing we can do."

"Talk to Adam Haliburton," said Laurie.

"Either he was expecting this envelope and we did miss it or someone wants to implicate him bad enough to plant it," Charles said. Charles struggled to stand and Laurie reached out to help him up. He turned and looked back toward the Haliburton property. It was only a short distance through the trees and downhill at that. "Can't we go this way?"

"Why?" asked Laurie.

"I'd much rather walk fifteen feet through the trees than up and around the bend. Following the road has to be at least four times the distance. Their drive is on the other side of the property." Charles pointed.

Laurie shrugged. "You're not having a very easy time of it are you? Alright, let's go this way."

Charles could tell that she wasn't thrilled about it but she could see his point. He wasn't having an easy time of it. Charles didn't like bringing it to Laurie's attention but in this case he was happy to sacrifice ego for practicality.

Their short walk through the bush led them to the side yard of the Haliburton house. Charles' feet were sore from the walk in the woods. The unstable ground hadn't done them any good but he was still sure that he would have been worse going back up to the road and all the way around. All he knew for sure was he would be glad when he was sitting down in the squad car and heading home. The closer he got to the side of the house the more he veered off toward the backyard. Something had caught his eye.

"Charles! What are you doing? Remember you're on private property. We have to go to the front door!" Laurie whispered as loudly as she could.

"Just come here, would you?" Charles was almost directly behind the house now. Directly in front of him was a large tarp—camouflaged for hunting. It was one of the extra large tarps that hunters set up. Actually, it seemed to have structure, maybe it was a tent? Charles thought. Charles reached down for the corner that was gathered beside the house just as Laurie reached his side. He stood pulling the camouflage tent with him. Underneath the tent was the red SUV.

"*Oh shit!*" Laurie said.

22

"Charles is this your truck?" Laurie hissed.

Charles shook his head with uncertainty. He couldn't believe what he was seeing. They had been searching for so long, now that it was right in front of him it didn't seem real or even possible—the glossy red paint, the chrome.

The tightness in his chest was back. He began to sweat. He wanted to run but he knew he couldn't. "I don't know. I have to see the front driver's side corner. It will be all smashed in."

"We have to get out of here *NOW!* There are too many coincidences surrounding this guy—he's your neighbour, there's a red SUV in his backyard covered by a camouflaged tarp, and he was just mailed what looks to be cocaine. We're going now!" Laurie pulled Charles into a standing position and the two of them headed back toward the car. They crossed the Haliburton lawn as softly as they could. If the bearded man was indeed Adam Haliburton then they were in no position to find him at home. Laurie needed to call for reinforcements before they pursued this any further.

Charles grabbed the handle on the passenger door of the cruiser and pulled it open. Wincing as he shifted his weight all onto one foot, he slipped as gracefully as he could into the car. Something didn't feel right. It was harder to get in than it should have been. "Why does the car feel so low?"

Laurie sat behind the wheel and reached for the car radio. She brought the handset toward her and the cord danced mockingly in the air. It had been cut. The frayed, rough end dangled over Laurie's lap. Charles and Laurie stared at each other in disbelief. Laurie swivelled the computer around to face her and began to type. She typed four letters before pulling her fingers back from the keyboard. She stared at them as if burned.

"What's the matter?" asked Charles.

"They're sticky," said Laurie. "Something has been poured all over the keyboard." She looked at the screen—it was blank, dark, and cracked. Laurie got out of the car and walked around it, inspecting it carefully. When she reached Charles' door she pulled it open and offered him her hand. "C'mon—let's go," she said.

"What?" Charles asked taking her hand.

"Someone's let all the air out of all four tires," she said.

Charles looked down at the wheels and sure enough they were all flat. They had been shredded by what would have had to be a fairly heavy knife.

"Let's head back to the rental house. We'll use the phone there to call Jeff," said Laurie. "I assume there is a land line there?"

Charles nodded. "In the kitchen."

The two of them made their way down Pondview Drive to the driveway of the rental house. Charles walked as fast as he could but he was finding it difficult to keep up with Laurie. He was holding her back and he knew it. "Laurie you go on ahead; I'll catch up," he said.

"No way. I'm not leaving you alone out here! Are you crazy? Just hurry up," Laurie said.

Once on the porch, Laurie reached for the front doorknob—it had been forced. The doorknob had been pried from the door. The lock box, that had held the key when they were there last, lay discarded on the porch. The wood door was splintered and ajar. They stopped and exchanged nervous glances. Laurie removed her gun from its holster.

Charles grabbed her arm. "He might still be in there!"

"Charles, I need that phone!" Laurie looked down at Charles' pockets. "Do you have your cell?"

276

Charles dug into his pocket and pulled out his cell phone. "Yes but a fat lot of good it will do us. The rental said that we have free wi-fi but we haven't since we moved in and the phone service out here sucks. I rarely get anything. When I called 9-1-1 when Jamie died, I used the landline."

"Shit!" Laurie said. "Well keep trying. We might get lucky."

Charles punched in 9-1-1 and hit *send*. *No Service* popped up on his screen. He hit *re-send*.

Laurie opened the front door wide enough to get in. She motioned for Charles to follow her. The two of them walked quietly into the living room. Laurie motioned for Charles to stay where he was as she continued into the kitchen. The kitchen, dining room, and living room made one big ell shape. Charles watched as Laurie reached for the goldenrod plastic phone fixed to the wall. She lifted the receiver and the cord bounced in sardonic imitation of the radio cord in the cruiser. Laurie replaced the handset a little harder than necessary. "Are there any other phones in the house?"

Charles shook his head. "I don't think so," he said. He looked at his cell again. There was a bar showing. He hit *send* again. *Calling* briefly lit the screen before switching to *Call Lost*. The bar left and was replaced with *No Service*. "What do we do now?"

A heavy thump emanated from another part of the house—the dull thud of a blunt object not the sharp crash of glass.

"That didn't come from upstairs," said Laurie.

"No, it didn't," said Charles. "It sounded like downstairs."

"There is no downstairs! You guys don't have a basement!" Laurie said incredulously.

"Well, not exactly but there is a cellar of sorts. You can't get to it from inside. There's a wooden door outside beside the shower but it's padlocked. We have never had the key," said Charles.

"Jesus Christ!" said Laurie. "So you have no idea what's down there?"

Charles shook his head. "None, I don't know why it didn't even occur to me."

"C'mon!" Laurie headed out the back door with Charles in pursuit. They rounded the house, past the pile of chopped wood, and stopped in front of the outdoor shower and wood double door to the cellar. The entrance was angled and the doors had been pulled open. Charles could see a set of dusty stone steps that led to an unfinished dirt floor.

Laurie looked at Charles. "Stay here. If you hear anything happen to me you run as fast as you can. If you see someone coming, call me like you don't know where I am—like you're looking for me. Got it?"

Charles nodded. "Be careful."

278

"You're a funny man," Laurie said. She looked briefly down the stairs and then turned quickly back to Charles. "I love you."

"Tell me tomorrow when you marry me," he smiled but then superstition got the better of him. "I love you too," he said.

Laurie descended the stairs cautiously. Charles crouched down at the corner of the door to get as much of a view of the cellar as possible. He could see most of it.

The cellar ran half the length of the house. It was stone, unfinished, and dusty. One side of the room was stocked with cardboard boxes that looked new and clean—certainly newer and cleaner than their surroundings. One box had toppled and split spilling hundreds of tiny plastic bags. Charles was too far away to read them but he could tell that they were the same bags that he had found in the envelope for Adam Haliburton marked *WHITE SHARK*. Charles watched Laurie walk deeper into the room. The further in she went, the shorter her shadow became. The only light was a single bare bulb that hung in the centre of the room. It was very bright. Laurie got deep enough that Charles could no longer see her head and neck. He tried to get lower but couldn't.

Laurie's body swivelled quickly to her right. She raised her gun but didn't fire. There was someone behind the boxes, out of Charles' line of vision. Charles could not see who it was. He heard a man's voice speak.

"I was wondering how long it would take you to get down here," the man said. "I had actually hoped that I would have this cleaned up before you did."

"Save it for the station," Charles heard Laurie say. "Let's go."

"I'm sorry about your car but I couldn't risk you calling for help," the man said.

"It's two against one—I'll be fine," said Laurie.

"But I called for help," the man said, "and my wingman is in a lot better shape than yours."

Charles strained to hear more when a car engine drowned out their conversation. Charles looked up to see a black SUV park at the top of the drive. The big man with the beard stepped out, slammed the driver's door harder than necessary, and headed down toward the house.

Charles' heart leapt in his chest. *If the man with the beard wasn't in the basement then who the hell was?* Charles crept backward to the woodpile and grabbed the biggest piece of firewood that he could manage. He retraced his steps past the cellar door and stepped into the outdoor shower. The shower stood between the cellar and the driveway. Charles stood with his back to the driveway and the bearded man. He listened as the big man plodded closer to the cellar, closer to Charles. Charles didn't dare turn around. He was sure that he hadn't been seen. Charles' heart pounded. He waited. He felt flush. All of the feelings from the closet came back. Charles gripped the thick slab of oak as hard as he could. Splinters dug into his fingers but he didn't care. He had to wait until he could see him. Charles could hear his heavy boots hitting the earth—closer and closer. Charles waited. The big man's shadow glided over the wood slats of the shower. Charles leapt out of his hiding spot. He swung the wood high and hard. The big man's skull cracked under the weight of the wood and the man fell to the bed of grass and pine needles like a felled tree. Charles stood over him wild-eyed and winded. He was prepared for the man to get up or at least to try but he didn't. He didn't move. Charles thought there would be a twitch in the man's extremities but there wasn't. Charles finally found his breath and oxygen screamed its way back into his lungs. It burned going down. Charles slid to the floor of the shower and sat there waiting for his heart to stop racing. Had he killed the man? There had been a definite and audible crack when Charles hit him. Charles had heard it and he had felt it. He had felt it reverberate up through his arms at the moment of impact. Maybe the bearded man was dead?

Charles turned his attention back to the basement. Laurie was still in there but with whom? Bracing himself on the doorframe, Charles descended the stairs. The bright light hit his eyes and made him squint. Laurie was in front of him.

"I told you to stay outside!" she said.

"The big bearded man is down and out. I might have killed him," Charles said. "At any rate, he's not going anywhere."

Charles walked further into the basement. He was far enough in to see Craig Phillips standing amidst the boxes of *WHITE SHARK* cocaine.

"Craig?" exclaimed Charles.

Reflexively, Laurie looked at Charles.

Craig took the distraction to throw a box of cocaine at Laurie. She stumbled as the tiny white bags flew at her face. Craig ran toward Charles and kicked him as hard as he could in the leg. Charles screamed and doubled over—he was falling. On his way down, Charles reached out and grabbed Craig at the waist. Craig was a thin man and Charles was able to link his left and right hands around him in a secure grip. Craig was not going anywhere without taking the deadweight of Charles with him. Charles pulled him down. Laurie was up and on top of Craig. She pulled his hands back behind him. He was cuffed before he even realised it. Charles let go of Craig and pulled himself up to his feet. His leg was throbbing from where Craig had kicked him but he didn't care. Charles wanted out of that basement. He made his way toward the basement door.

When Craig Phillips was walked out of the cellar in handcuffs, Charles was sitting on the shower floor. Charles was sure he would have long fallen over had he not been. Craig looked at the big man—who was still lying facedown in the dirt—then turned to Charles and grinned. "Well, haven't you been busy," he said.

Laurie looked at the big man and then at Charles. "Is he dead?"

Charles shook his head. "I don't know yet. I was just about to check him for identification."

"Throw these on him first," Laurie said throwing a pair of handcuffs at Charles.

Charles pulled the bearded man's hands back behind him and cuffed him. The cuffs barely fit around his wrists. Charles then reached into the rear pocket of the man's jeans and pulled out a wallet. He read his driver's licence aloud.

"Louis Grover?" said Charles.

"What?" asked Laurie.

"That's what it says—*Louis Grover.*"

"Who the hell is Louis Grover?" asked Laurie.

"I've never heard of him," said Craig Phillips.

"I'm sure," said Laurie irritably. "Damn it, Craig— I can't tell you how disappointed I am that you're responsible for all of this crap!"

"Louis Grover is Sam Grover's father," said Charles.

"How do you know that?" asked Laurie.

"Violet told Jeff and me when we went to visit her," Charles said.

"Jesus Christ," Laurie exclaimed. "Is he alive? Please tell me he's alive."

Charles felt the Louis's wrist until he found a pulse. "There's a pulse. It's weak but it's there."

"You stay here. I'll be right back," Laurie said. Laurie walked Craig Phillips up to the squad car and locked him in the backseat. Then she came back down to Charles. "Okay, I'm going to stay here with him. You drive that SUV into town, call Jeff and tell him I'm out here, get an ambulance for Louis Grover, and get an officer to drop you at my place. Alright?"

"I can do that," Charles said as Laurie helped him to his feet. "Will you be alright?"

"Oh sure, I'll be fine," Laurie said. "Craig's locked in the back. He's not going anywhere. I'll just wait here and keep an eye on Louis."

"Okay," Charles said. Charles got into the black SUV that Louis Grover drove up in and was grateful to find out that it was an automatic. He turned around and drove down Pondview leaving Laurie with the two handcuffed men. Charles was still trying to play it out in his mind. Why would Sam Grover's father—Louis Grover—want Charles dead? Why would he kill his own son? How would he get a hold of his son's cocaine to cut it with strychnine?

Charles followed Barnes Road to Wing Road and eventually Circuit Avenue into Oak Bluffs central. Jeff was walking out of Mocha Mott's carrying a coffee when Charles saw him. He beeped his horn repeatedly until Jeff realised who he was. Charles stopped and Jeff walked over to his window.

"Where'd you get the wheels?" Jeff asked.

"Laurie is at the Pondview house. She has Craig Phillips and Louis Grover in custody. Louis is going to need an ambulance; when I left he was unconscious."

"Why did she arrest Craig Phillips of all people," Jeff exclaimed. "Where the hell did Louis Grover come from?"

"Craig has been dealing drugs and Louis Grover is the big man with the beard," said Charles. "I'm not sure exactly what the story is yet. Laurie and Craig were in the basement when they were doing most of their talking."

"Why would Sam Grover's father want you dead?" asked Jeff. "Never mind, I'll get out there to Laurie and call in assistance. You drive yourself to Laurie's house and stay there. Alright?"

"Okay." Charles drove toward East Chop deep in thought. As he turned up East Chop drive, an ambulance whipped by him in full siren. It was the first time that Charles actually remembered finding comfort in the sound of an ambulance. He and Laurie had done it. They had closed the case. They didn't know the details yet—at least Charles didn't—but they had the culprits all but behind bars and they had done it all before lunch. For the first time that day, Charles noticed he was starving.

23

Laurie walked in the front door and dropped her things on the kitchen counter. Charles woke with a start. He had given himself a sponge bath when he got in, taken off a lot of his bandages, and then fallen asleep on the couch with a glass of wine. Laurie found herself a wine glass and pulled out the bottle of Kim Crawford Sauvignon Blanc that Charles had already opened. Laurie poured the wine not to the traditional widest part of the bowl but rather she filled her glass to the top. She then walked into the den and sat beside Charles. She took a double swallow.

"So, how was your day?" asked Charles.

"Swell," she chuckled.

"What did Craig Phillips have to say for himself?" he asked.

"Not much. Louis Grover is in a coma," said Laurie. "So until he wakes up, all we have on Craig is possession with intent to distribute."

"That's it?" asked Charles.

"Well, he'll get jail time for that but not much with a good lawyer and he can afford one. Did you know he owns that rental property?"

"No, I didn't," said Charles.

"Neither did I. There's nothing else to connect him to anything, at least not yet. Especially with a witness," Laurie said.

"Who?"

"You, Charles! You have already gone on record saying that you saw Louis Grover kill Jamie and you've told me that he was the same man who tried to kill you in the red SUV. There's nothing to connect Craig Phillips to any of that."

"I suppose you're right."

"There's nothing or no one to connect Louis to Craig either," said Laurie. Laurie gulped her wine again. "I need something to eat. Why don't I barbeque us some burgers?"

Just as Laurie stood, the phone rang. She walked over to the kitchen and picked it up. "Hello?" Laurie paused while the person on the other end spoke. "I'll be right there," she said. Laurie hung up the phone and turned to look at Charles. "You'll want to come with me."

*   *   *

Laurie parked the car in the parking lot of the Martha's Vineyard Hospital very close to where she had parked that morning. The sun was higher now, it was much later in the day, and the hospital was a lot busier than it had been on their previous visit. Instead of going in the main door, Laurie led Charles toward the emergency entrance. The automatic sliding glass doors parted when they got close and a wall of cool air greeted them.

"Hi, Chief!" said Connie.

"Connie, don't you ever go home?" asked Laurie.

"You know what they say, *no rest for the weary!*" Connie smiled. "Are you here to see Jack Burrell again? I don't think he's awake yet."

"No, we're not. Would you page Doctor Elkins for me please? She's expecting us," said Laurie.

"Oh certainly, Chief. Shall I tell her what it's about?" Connie asked with just a little too much curiosity.

"As I said, Connie, she's expecting us. Thanks again."

Charles sat down in one of the lobby chairs but Laurie remained standing. Almost immediately, Dr Elkins appeared and walked over to shake Laurie's hand. "Thank you for coming, Chief Knickles. Please, follow me."

Charles stood up and followed Laurie and Dr Elkins to a hospital room. The room was small but bright. It was more or less the same as the other rooms that Charles had seen in that hospital. This room had one bed that was occupied by a very thin but beautiful black woman. She turned and looked at the three of them when they entered. She smiled. Charles knew right away who she was. The high cheekbones, the delicate nose, and high forehead, the features were younger but unmistakeable.

"If you don't need me for anything right now, I have a few things to do. I'll leave you to it. Call if you need me," said Dr Elkins.

"Thank you, doctor," said the woman in the bed. "Chief Knickles, I am Carla Beacham."

"Ms Beacham, I think I should ask you if you want a lawyer present," said Laurie.

"No thank you," said Carla.

"Then what can I do for you?" asked Laurie. "I must admit, I have a few questions of my own."

"The doctor tells me that there is very little chance that my husband, Louis, will never wake up."

"I don't know. I haven't talked to anybody recently about his condition," said Laurie. "I know he's in a coma—I'm sorry."

"Chief, it's important to me that you know what happened, that you know why Louis did what he did. That's why I called for you."

Laurie didn't say anything, just waited for Carla to continue.

"Chief, Craig Phillips was blackmailing my husband into working for him. Craig was trafficking drugs and using my husband to distribute for him and act as a collector. It started small...slowly got to be more and more...bigger deliveries, bigger collections. You don't slip into this kind of thing overnight. It creeps up on you slowly like quick sand. You don't realise you're up to your neck in it until you are." Carla looked sad and maybe, thought Charles, a little embarrassed.

"Why should I believe you, Ms Beacham? Why would Mr Phillips do such a thing? I'm not saying you're lying; however, I do know that Craig Phillips is going to be able to enlist several character witnesses and a very expensive lawyer. I'm going to need more than your word, ma'am," Laurie sat down in a chair beside Carla's bed.

"Chief Knickles, I am HIV positive. That's why I came back. I wanted to see my son before I was too sick, before I couldn't travel. Craig Phillips was paying my husband in prescription drugs. My treatments cost five thousand dollars a month. Do you have that kind of money to spend on pills? I don't have that kind of money. I did have some money that my father left me but it didn't last very long."

"When did you contract HIV, Ms Beacham?" asked Laurie. "People can live long productive lives with HIV these days."

"During my pregnancy with Samuel. When he was born, he was given zidovudine and when he passed his second negative test, they took him away from me—rather my mother took him away. Violet convinced me that since I could not even breastfeed him that he would be better off with her than with Louis and me. Violet said that I would make my boy sick again. She said that if he stayed with me, that we would both wind up dead. Violet even convinced me that it would be better for me—easier for me to take care of myself and not to have to look at a baby that I could barely touch. I was a damned fool."

"That was not the story that Violet told us," said Charles.

"I'm sorry, who are you?" asked Carla.

"Carla, this is my fiancé, Charles Williams. He ended up much deeper in this case than he would have liked," said Laurie.

"I see. I'm sure it wasn't what she told you, Mr Williams, but if it makes you feel any better, I'm sure that Violet believes that what she told you was God's own truth," Carla shook her head. "That woman's twisted her mind up with so many lies, she has to screw her hat on in the morning." Carla laughed until she coughed and began to choke. Laurie reached for a glass of water and passed it to her. She sipped it until her breathing returned to normal. "Anyway, Chief if you follow the drugs—my drugs, you'll find the truth. I still have some that I haven't taken yet. Prescriptions leave a trail not like cocaine. Pass me my purse please."

Laurie leaned down and pulled her purse out from under the nightstand and handed it to her.

Carla reached in and pulled out a small white box of prescription drugs. "Follow those. He got them out of Florida from someone near his old house. I'm not sure where that is exactly but that's why he moved. Follow those—that will connect my husband to Craig Phillips."

"My husband is a good man, Chief Knickles, but he made some mistakes. Selling drugs is a horrible business. It changed Louis. He let that Craig Phillips get the best of him but he did it because he loved me. I don't know how to feel about that. He didn't want me to die. I know that I would have done anything for him if the roles were reversed." Carla's eyes glassed over and she turned to the window.

"That doesn't excuse murder, Ms Beacham," said Laurie.

"What?" asked Carla.

"Your husband killed a young man, shot a police officer, and tried to kill my fiancé with his red SUV."

"No, ma'am, he did not!" Carla stiffened in bed. A strength appeared in her that hadn't been there a moment ago. Charles was reminded of his visit to Violet. It was that same fire. *"I invited you here to tell you the truth!* My Louis made some mistakes and I don't mind telling you because there is nothing anyone can do to him now. His fate is in God's hands but Louis never killed anyone! He couldn't—it wasn't in his nature! Does a man who loves his wife and wants to see her live so badly kill another man? I don't think so. He never even drove that red SUV—not once! He's never even been inside it! You won't find any of his prints in that red truck when you find it. That SUV belongs to Craig Phillips! That house you found the drugs in belongs to Craig Phillips—he owns the house beside it too!" Carla looked over to Charles. "That was you he tried to run over? I'm sorry, I didn't know. If I'd known that, I would have said something up front. I only heard that story in bits and pieces. I figured he was trying to take out some other drug dealer and that would not be any of my business." Carla looked at Charles and looked as if she was going to speak again but the light in her eyes began to fade and she slumped back onto her pillows. "I'm tired now, Chief Knickles, Mr Williams. I think I have to ask you to leave." Carla Beacham pushed the button for the nurse and the nurse came in with a promptness that Charles would not have thought possible.

Charles and Laurie walked out into the hall to find Dr Elkins waiting for them.

"Did that help?" asked the doctor.

"I think so," Laurie said. "She might have hung herself in the process I'm afraid. I'm not sure yet."

"She'll be long dead before it goes to trial," said the doctor.

"How long does she have?" asked Laurie.

"Not long," said Dr Elkins. "Have a good day."

Laurie and Charles walked back out of the hospital into the sunshine. When they were both outside and sure they were out of earshot, Laurie turned to Charles, "I thought you said you got a clear look at the man who shot Jack and tried to kill you at my house?"

"I did!" Charles exclaimed. "I know it was night but it was a clear night—the moon was out and it was bright! I saw a big man in a plaid jacket—you know we used to call them North Bay dinner jackets—those red, plaid wool things? A trucker hat and a beard."

"We need to get a better look at that truck," said Laurie.

*   *   *

Charles and Laurie stepped out of the car back at the Pondview house. This time it was not a quiet bucolic scene but a swarm of police behind a barrier of yellow police tape.

"Stay here," Laurie said as she ducked under the tape and walked down the drive. She returned a few moments later with Jeff in tow.

"Hey, Charles, how are you feeling?" asked Jeff.

"Pretty good thanks. How's it going in there?"

"Crazy. That's a lot of drugs," Jeff said. "Craig will be going away for a while; I don't care who his lawyer is. So where are you taking me?"

"Next door," said Laurie.

"Why?" asked Jeff.

"I have a surprise for you!" said Laurie.

The three of them walked in silence down the drive of the neighbouring house and walked around back. The tarp was still there and the corner still lifted where Charles had peeked underneath. The gleaming red metal was well exposed.

"Holy! Is that what I think it is? Is that your truck, Charles? A red Jeep Cherokee—old one too," Jeff said.

"Help me get this tarp off," asked Laurie. Jeff and Laurie each grabbed a corner and pulled back the tarp. The Jeep Cherokee had tinted windows and one damaged corner on the driver's side.

"That's it. That's my truck," said Charles.

Laurie lifted the door handle and the door opened. "Well, isn't that convenient?"

296

"Why would he leave the doors unlocked?" marvelled Charles.

"It was under a camouflage tarp; why lock a truck that you don't think anyone is going to find?" said Laurie.

"That's stupid," said Jeff.

"That's arrogance," said Charles.

"*Holy shit!*" exclaimed Laurie. "There's a red plaid jacket back here layered over another sweater, two pairs of jeans—one inside the other, a trucker hat, and this!" Laurie reached behind the driver seat and produced a beard.

"He was setting Louis Grover up!"

"Well, he just hung himself." Laurie put the beard back down. "Jeff, if you don't mind, I'm going to take Charles home."

"No problem—I got this," Jeff grinned. "I'll see you guys tomorrow."

"You'd better believe it!" Charles said. "See? Aren't you glad that we're still getting married? We need this now more than ever. If Craig Phillips had ruined our wedding on top of everything else, you would never have gotten over it...and neither would I."

"You're right," Laurie said.

"I am?"

"Don't get used to it—that ends tomorrow."

24

Charles and Laurie were outside on the back deck. Laurie was standing in front of the barbeque poking at her homemade beef patties and Charles was sitting in a greyed Adirondack chair reading *Murder On The Orient Express* by Agatha Christie. They were both nursing glasses of the Kim Crawford Sauvignon Blanc full of ice.

"I would have thought you'd read that already," said Laurie. She flipped all three patties and they sizzled as the raw meat hit the grill. The sides she turned up were done to ruddy brown perfection each with a set of black grill marks burned in.

"I have," said Charles. "It's a good book."

"But you already know who did it?" Laurie said. She took some wine and sucked some ice into her mouth. She crunched the cubes.

"It's still a good book," Charles insisted.

"I guess," said Laurie.

Charles looked at the grill. "Why do you always do that?"

"Do what?" asked Laurie.

"Cook an extra burger or patty or steak?"

"Well, you might want another one," she said.

"You're right—I might want another one but I'll never need another one. I swear I'm going to get huge married to you! The burgers smell awesome though…"

"Thanks!" Laurie leaned in to kiss Charles but before she could, Jeff walked around the back corner of the house.

"Hey!" Jeff called. "I figured you guys would be back here."

"I thought we weren't seeing you until tomorrow," said Laurie.

Charles gave her a sideways glance and then looked back to Jeff. "Not that you're not welcome! Jesus, Laurie."

"Are you on duty, Jeff?" asked Laurie.

"Yeah, kinda," he said.

"Alright. Out with it," Laurie said.

"Violet Beacham is dead," Jeff blurted.

Charles and Laurie said nothing. They looked at each other. Laurie took her hamburgers off the heat.

"There's more," Jeff said. "It looks like it was suicide."

"Aw shit," Laurie said.

"That's awful," said Charles.

"She left a note." Jeff offered the envelope that he was carrying to Laurie. "I made a copy; I thought you'd want to see it."

"I don't know if *want* is the right word..." Laurie sighed and took the envelope delicately. She opened it and pulled out the photocopy. She read in silence. Then without looking up, she read it again aloud.

'Carla,

I know you are on the island, Samuel told me. I don't blame you for not wanting to see me, Carla—I took away your child. I thought I was doing right by you at the time. This is such a small island, Carla. I couldn't imagine what people would say about you having a baby and having that horrible disease. How would they have treated you, Carla? How would they have treated Samuel? So, I took Samuel away from you. The irony is that taking your child away from you left me childless. I lost my Carla. I pushed you away and resented Samuel for it. I know I did. I resented him so

300

I took it out on him and that made me resent him even more. He deserved better. Samuel was a good boy. He was a good boy, Carla, until he got mixed up in those drugs. Your Samuel was a good boy. I could not stand by and watch him lose his soul to those drugs. So I sent him to God before he sent himself to hell. I mixed rat poison into some drugs I found in his pocket. I figured maybe he wouldn't feel it then. I know what I did was a sin but I sacrificed my soul for Samuel. That gives me some peace. They say the road to hell is paved with good intentions. Well, I guess I am going to find out quicker than most.

Love,

Violet (Mum)'

Laurie looked up at Charles and Jeff. There were tears beading on her eyelashes. "Did you give it to Carla?"

Jeff shook his head. "I tried but she wouldn't take it."

"Maybe you shouldn't," said Charles.

"What difference does it make at this point?" asked Laurie. "Her whole family is gone. Christ, the whole thing is awful."

"Knowing your mother really did love you before you pass yourself is a very big deal," said Charles.

"That's true but at what cost? Violet killed her grandson. I think I could go my whole life without knowing that my mother killed my son after forcing me to live apart from him. The whole thing makes me feel nauseous," said Laurie. "Damn, I was so glad that this whole thing was all over. I was enjoying my evening so much and now this." Laurie turned back to the barbeque and put the burgers back on the grill.

None of them said anything for several minutes. Charles was mulling over his opinion of Violet Beacham and he assumed the others were doing the same. Violet had always come across as an angry and bitter woman. It made her easy to dismiss as a crank. Charles had done just that. He had seen her as an island busy body that had too much time on her hands. It had been impossible to see that she walked around with the knowledge that she had destroyed three lives—hers, her daughter's, and her grandson's—and she didn't know how to get far enough around her own pride to fix them.

"Will you stay for a burger, Jeff?" Laurie asked solemnly. "There's one extra."

"Sure, I'd like that," Jeff said.

The three of them sat in silence.

25

Charles walked though the bedroom fastening the cufflink on his dress shirt. He thought he looked pretty good. He was wearing a simple navy suit with a white shirt and a red tie. All his American friends would think he was trying to assimilate nicely but he knew in his heart of hearts—they were his *JAWS* colours. Charles had chosen shoes and a belt in a caramel brown. He looked in the mirror at what he had created. He did think that he looked good but he didn't think that he looked like himself. It was weird to see himself dressed up. Charles always thought that people put a little too much weight in this sort of thing but that was that. If you want to marry a pretty girl, you have to buy a pretty outfit...and Laurie Knickles was indeed a pretty girl. Charles wasn't sure why she wanted to marry him. He wasn't exactly sure why she even wanted to talk to him half the time. He was kind of funny. Actually, women said that a lot. Men should consider themselves damned lucky that women found it attractive when men were funny because most of them didn't have a whole lot else going for them. All in all, they tended to be a self-absorbed lot and kind of smelly. Charles hated cologne and he usually found the men who wore it to be pretty obnoxious. After his shower, he had moisturized with Hawaiian Tropic sunscreen; it made him smell like coconut. That was as far as he was willing to go. He ran his hand through his hair; it always looked kind of tousled. His dark tan made his green eyes glow. Charles took a deep breath. He was as ready as he would ever be. He left the bedroom and walked down the stairs to the front foyer of Laurie's house.

Brad was waiting for him just inside the front door. "I thought I was going to have to go up and get you!" he said.

"Are we late?" asked Charles.

"No. We're fine," assured Brad. He led Charles out of the house and closed the front door behind them. "Where are you guys going for your honeymoon?"

"Nantucket," said Charles.

"*Seriously?*" Brad asked as he slipped behind the wheel of his green Subaru Outback.

"Seriously!" said Charles. "We thought about going somewhere else—you know the usual spots—but we both think this is the most beautiful place there is. If we go to Nantucket, she doesn't have to be chief of police. We rented a beach house—we can *both* be tourists!"

"You live in a beach house on Martha's Vineyard and for your honeymoon, you're renting a beach house on Nantucket," Brad rolled his eyes. "You guys crack me up." Brad put the Subaru in gear and drove down East Chop Drive toward The Edgartown Inn.

*　　*　　*

Charles stepped out of the car onto the gravel parking lot of The Edgartown Library. A wall of greenery separated the library from the inn and Charles could hear the laughter and chatter of his wedding guests emanating from beyond it. He and Brad took the few steps necessary on North Water Street to get to the front steps of the inn and made their way up. As if on cue, the door swung open and Edie met them at the top.

"Edie, you look beautiful!" exclaimed Charles.

"Well, you don't have to sound so surprised!" Edie said.

"I'm not! Quite the contrary! I'm wondering if I chose the right woman!" teased Charles.

"Oh for crying out loud!" Edie scolded him but the blush of her cheeks said she loved every minute of it.

"That blue is really stunning on you. You really do look gorgeous."

"Well, you didn't think that I was going to wear black to your wedding did you?" Edie took his lapel in one hand and a rose from the table just inside the door with the other. She held a pin between her lips and mumbled, "Hold still." With the rose in place, she took the pin and fastened it like a pro.

Charles looked at Edie and his eyes glassed over. He felt his face flush. "Thank you for doing this for us, Edie."

"You look very handsome," Edie said—ignoring him.

"We love you very much you know," Charles continued unwavering.

Edie looked up and dabbed at her eyes with a tissue. "Oh, for God's sake, Charles! What are you trying to do to me? I'm going to go in there looking like a raccoon!"

Charles reached down, took Edie by the shoulders, and kissed her on the cheek.

"Alright, that's enough now. I love you too!" Edie dabbed at her eyes and straightened her dress. "I'm going to be in such a state!" She looked at Brad. "Take him in to the dining room but no further."

306

Brad and Charles walked into the dining room to find it filled to the brim with food. The tables had been rearranged so that people could walk through quickly and easily to get their meals buffet style but the tables weren't set up how Charles remembered Edie and Laurie discussing. The tablecloth was blue at the front and tan at the back and there were little red and white striped tents lined up along the back. Charles didn't know what those were for. Maybe there were salads underneath them? Charles had to admit that he hadn't been paying one hundred percent attention but he thought that he had been paying close enough attention that he knew what was going on! Clearly he hadn't. Laurie walked into the dining room from the inn and walked up to Charles.

"Hey!" Charles looked her up and down. He couldn't remember ever seeing anyone ever look that beautiful. It was almost confusing. Do people really look like that? Charles wouldn't have thought it to be possible. How did someone ache so happily like he did at that moment? There was no way to explain it. "You look beautiful," he said and felt foolish for saying it. It didn't begin to describe what he was feeling.

"Thank you. For the record, I wouldn't mind seeing a little more of this side of you either," she smiled and kissed him.

"The shorts and Nike Shox aren't cutting it anymore?" he asked.

Laurie shrugged playfully.

"I thought I was going to be in the garden and you were going to walk out to me? You know, down the aisle and all of that," Charles asked.

Laurie looked at Edie and back at Charles. "Yeah, about that, there's been a bit of a smoke and mirror thing going on here," she said.

"There has? Who's perpetrated this ruse?" asked Charles.

Edie put her hand up and Laurie grinned guiltily.

"Is that why I don't recognise the table set-up in here?" asked Charles.

"Do you like it?" asked Laurie.

"I think I'm missing something," Charles said.

"You'll figure it out in a minute," said Edie. "Okay, Laurie, they're ready."

Charles offered Laurie his arm and Laurie took it. Taking the door slightly sideways, they slipped through to the back garden of The Edgartown Inn or what Charles remembered as the garden of the Edgartown Inn. What they really stepped into was Amity Island circa 1975.

A large banner painted to look like the billboard from *JAWS* hung from the balcony of the Edgartown Inn cottage. The yellow border, the woman on the water raft, and the big letters that read *Amity Island Welcomes You* was the first thing Charles saw. "Holy cow!" Charles blurted out without thinking. The small crowd laughed.

Charles' eyes darted quickly around the room. Each table had a white tablecloth with a centrepiece in the middle. The flowers in each centrepiece were red and white and arranged to look like a life preserver—a twelve inch laminated cardboard cut-out of a JAWS character stood out of each one. There was a Brody table, a Hooper table, a Quint table, an Ellen Brody table, and a Mayor Vaughn table. Last but not least, there was a Mrs Taft table. Charles pointed at the Mrs Taft cardboard cutout and laughed. "That's awesome!"

"She is your favourite," Laurie said squeezing his arm.

Charles turned to the head table to see a two and a half foot maquette of Bruce the Shark taking centre stage. "That's the Sideshow Collectibles Maquette!"

"That's your wedding present from me," Laurie said. "I know you don't have one."

"I thought we weren't getting each other wedding presents?" Charles looked at her—briefly losing his smile.

"Did you get me a present?" she asked.

"Yes," he said. His smile returned just a little more wickedly than when it had left.

"So what's my present?" asked Laurie.

Charles turned toward the inn and called out, "Okay, Jeff!"

The entire wedding party stood and applauded as Jeff and Chris wheeled Sergeant Jack Burrell's wheelchair down onto the grass. Jack waved as Jeff bumped him down from the backdoor of the inn. Laurie ran over to him and knelt before his chair. Laurie was crying now. Her face wet with tears. "Jack! Are you okay? Should you even be here?"

"Dr Elkins was a bit iffy at first but when I reminded her that Dr Beller was going to be here, she relented," Jeff said.

"Oh, I'm so glad that she did," Laurie leaned in and hugged Jack. "I'm so glad you're okay, Jack."

"Me too! Thanks for asking Jeff to come and get me! I was really upset when I thought I was going to miss it. I love weddings. I went to them all the time when I was a kid. Did I ever tell you that I got drunk when I was ten at a wedding? It was my uncle's—"

"Take him over to Mrs Taft's table," said Charles. Charles stood up straight. He looked at Laurie. "I just got it!" he said. "The buffet table is State Beach, isn't it?"

"Yup," she said. "And after dinner, we're all watching *JAWS!*"

"*Oi! Let's get this show on the road you two!*" Brooke yelled from the Brody table.

Hand in hand, Charles and Laurie walked to the back of the garden and stood in front of the Humanist.

310

"Do you, Charles Williams, take Laurie Knickles to be your wife?" asked the Humanist.

"I do." Charles slipped the wedding band on Laurie's finger.

"And do you, Laurie Knickles, take Charles Williams to be your husband?" asked the Humanist.

"I do." Laurie slipped the matching band on Charles' ring finger.

"Then by the power in me, I now pronounce you husband and wife."

Charles grabbed Laurie by the shoulders and Laurie kissed him with all of her strength. It had all been worth it. The crowd cheered and applauded. When they broke apart, Laurie's face was wet with tears.

Charles didn't think he would ever stop smiling.

Fin.

312

Made in the USA
Middletown, DE
06 January 2019